Problems
with People

Problems with People

stories

DAVID GUTERSON

ALFRED A. KNOPF
New York
2014

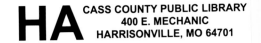

THIS IS A BORZOI BOOK
PUBLISHED BY ALFRED A. KNOPF

www.aaknopf.com

Knopf, Borzoi Books, and the colophon are registered trademarks of Random House LLC.

Selected stories in this work originally appeared in the following: "Hush" and "Paradise" in *The American Scholar;* "Shadow" in *Boulevard;* "Photograph" as "The Drowned Son" in *Harper's;* "Pilanesberg" in *The Indiana Review;* "Hot Springs" in *Narrative;* "Tenant" in *The New England Review;* and "Politics" in *ZYZZYVA.*

Grateful acknowledgment is made to Alfred Music for permission to reprint an excerpt from "Not to Touch the Earth," words and music by the Doors. Copyright © 1968 (Renewed) Doors Music Co. All Rights Reserved. Reprinted by permission of Alfred Music.

Library of Congress Cataloging-in-Publication Data
Guterson, David.
   [Short stories. Selections]
   Problems with People : Stories / David Guterson. — First Edition.
      pages   cm
   ISBN 978-0-385-35148-5 (hardcover : alk. paper) —
   ISBN 978-0-385-35149-2 (eBook)
   I. Title
   PS3557.U846A6 2014   813'.54—dc23   2013029700

Jacket photograph: *Untitled #163,* 2011, from the series
"Until the Kingdom Comes" by Simen Johan,
courtesy of Yossi Milo Gallery, New York
Jacket design by Kelly Blair

Manufactured in the United States of America
First Edition

To Charles Johnson

Contents

Problems
with People

Paradise

They went in late September, starting out on I-5, which she handled by staying in the right lane with ample braking distance, keeping her hands at nine and three on the wheel, and disdaining speeders and tailgaters. No problem there—he found her driving style charming enough. She was a silver beauty in a dark-blue Honda Element—one of those boxy, hip-to-be-square cars—with nearly inaudible public-radio chatter on fade, and all of that was fine, too. She wore a jean jacket with mother-of-pearl buttons, an ironed pastel skirt, and suede lace sandals. Her eyes were green, her smile was warm, and she didn't talk just to fill space. She seemed self-sufficient but not cold about it. In her politics, she was not so liberal as to be obnoxious, but not so conservative as to suggest one-upmanship. She didn't pretend to be an organic farmer, kitchen goddess, world traveler, yoga master, or humanitarian; neither was she reactionary with regard to those personas. She was green but not gloomy and, though not indifferent to approaching sixty, not obsessed by it, either. She had a good sense of humor—quiet and subtle. She didn't expect to live forever via exercise and a healthy diet. She understood that he was still in the aftermath—damaged goods—without making it central to the way she treated him. In short, so far he wasn't disenchanted. But he still expected to be.

How had this happened—this trip to Paradise? Via match.com, that was the simple answer. The idea that he would need match.com—he wouldn't have predicted it, hadn't seen that he would go there. But match.com was what people did now, and actually, it made sense. It saved single people trouble and grief, decreased their disappointments and misunderstandings. Digitalized, you put yourself out there, minus the pretense that it was other than what it was. You cut to the chase without preliminaries. And the people you met were just like you—they'd also resorted to match.com—so you didn't have to feel embarrassed, really, unless you wanted to do that together and mutually laugh at yourselves.

They'd skipped that step—the self-loathing self-punctures—opting instead for straightforwardness in a wine bar, where he told her immediately about his wife, and she told him about her former husband, long remarried. He described his children—a boy out of college and a girl still in, both thousands of miles from him—and she described her energetic twin sons, who'd found good marriage partners, stayed in Seattle, and started a successful business together, selling "hand-forged" donuts. He knew about her work from her match.com profile, but asked about it anyway, as a matter of course: sociology at Seattle University, and doing research, right now, on social networks and epidemiology. His turn arrived: commercial litigation, specializing in securities fraud. What exactly was securities fraud? And so they got through their first date.

Their second—which he initiated, though the first had been arduous and painful—was for an early dinner and Russian chamber music. Russian chamber music was her idea, something she had enough of an interest in to have accepted, gratis, two tickets from a colleague; they might as well go, why not, they agreed, since neither knew the first thing about Russian chamber music but both were willing to find out about it. At dinner in a warehouse full of people half their age, he discovered that his date was allergic to peanuts, a light eater, and a morning lap swimmer. The World Health Organization, in conjunction with FIND—Foundation for Innovative New Diagnostics—had sent her during her sabbatical, last year, to study sleeping sickness in Uganda. No, she hadn't traveled elsewhere in Africa, but she had gone to Geneva for a WHO convention in the middle of her Ugandan research, and to Dublin on her way home to see a friend with ALS. Dublin was a subject he could talk about a little. He'd played semi-pro basketball in Cork for three seasons. A minor sport there—give them hurling instead. What's hurling? she wondered genially. Golf without rules, he replied.

Did he play golf, then? Never, he assured her. Golf courses, they agreed, were a waste of water, although, like cemeteries, they relieved the eye of urban density. What, then? For exercise? He rode a bicycle to work five days a week. He confessed to dressing like a bike nerd to do it—the polyester jersey, the Lycra shorts, the waterproof helmet cover, the fingerless gloves.

The fluorescent, high-visibility colors. The weekend racer's flourishes and trim. Was all of that a mistake? He couldn't tell. Self-deprecation could easily backfire. Calling yourself a geek: surely counterproductive. He shut up about bicycling and engaged her on politics: what did she think about tearing down the viaduct and replacing it with a tunnel through downtown Seattle? They ate, split the bill, and walked toward the chamber music: twilight in the city, just a little car breeze; a waif with ANYTHING HELPS scrawled on cardboard. "Maybe," he thought, "my chinos are wrong," but she hadn't really dressed up, either—black with a little sparkle in her sweater. Still, she had that notable feature—the lustrous head of bobbed silver hair—that would cover her when semi-formal was required, as it might be required for Russian chamber music.

As it turned out, he didn't love or hate the chamber music, had no strong feelings one way or the other about the string quartet and attractive young pianist playing Rachmaninoff and Shostakovich, but he did notice something in Benaroya Hall that spurred him toward a third date. Sitting beside this new and unfamiliar woman in box seats over a corner of the proscenium, he was keenly aware of her well-coiffed hair, her straight carriage, and her hands in her lap, and he found himself excited. And scared.

Their third date was for dinner at an Italian restaurant that afforded plenty of privacy. There they broached sex in plain, honest terms. He told her he didn't know what would happen in bed. He said he hadn't slept with anyone but his wife for twenty-six years—then add on the six months since she'd died of a heart attack while in the middle of leaving him for someone new.

Mount Rainier was cloud-bound, cloaked, helmeted, gone. The new woman in his life got off I-5 at Fife and did battle with Puyallup—its traffic lights, turn lanes, and arterial aggressiveness—by dint of the same methodical approach that had seen her through the freeway's fury. She showed no sign of needing the right coffee shop, missing her cell phone, or worrying a list in her head. She didn't deplore the South Hill Mall, or either of the Walmart Supercenters they passed, or the growth of Graham, or clear-cuts. Nor did she make a big deal about the apples being picked by ladder climbers wearing vest bags, or the scarlet vine-maple leaves right now at their best, or roadside fruit stands. They passed through a stretch of low-lying fog, small farms, lakes, and alder thickets. Here the light was even more dour, and the pastures were clammy, hoofed down to mud. Was that worth talking about? Was it corny and off-putting to be enamored of the fall landscape, even in a muted and prosaic way? Should he talk about these matters—fall and its merits, fall and its sadness, fall and the perils in too much description of it—or should he go on saying nothing, play it safe? Silence didn't seem exactly right, but he felt hamstrung and chastised by his own mental chatter. Maybe it was better not to talk.

It rained in earnest. There were no cute towns, just trailers and blight, mini-marts and badly named burger joints. They entered Mount Rainier National Park and, on the road to Paradise, walked to Narada Falls beneath umbrellas. Now she, too, had little to say. They were both silent, watching the waterfall in the rain. Driving again, she set her teeth against her lower lip. The rain-pelted slopes of the mountain came into view, and the last of the blue September gentians, wind-whipped. The lodge was as advertised—grand and hand-crafted, rustic and Gothic, simple but complicated, well appointed but crude. It seemed to him a massive mistake, everything too big, too lodgelike in earnest. He kept this to himself, though. He felt scattered, apprehensive. They checked in on two credit cards and went to their room—a standard with a queen bed, no television, no phone—at the end of the hall on the fourth floor of the annex, with a view of the Tatoosh Range, weather permitting. But right now, the weather didn't permit.

I might as well be open, he said, taking the room's one chair, a wooden desk chair. I'm nervous.

Me, too.

I'm losing my cool. Could we pull the shades? It's me I don't want to see, not you. I don't want to look at myself right now. No, I'm not going to whine the whole time, I promise, but—

Sure.

It's time, he said. Thank you.

He stooped to unzip the bag he'd brought, reached in, and told her, I thought I might—you know—need this. He showed her a bottle of pills.

Okay.

Excuse me. Just for a minute.

He went into the bathroom and took the pill with water. Privacy allowed him to agitate his doubts and shore himself up simultaneously. Who if not her? But this was a mistake. His wife was gone, but this was too sudden. Quietly, he brushed his teeth, then came back to find her in the chair with her handbag settled and open in her lap. While he'd been in the bathroom, she'd drawn the shades; there was no more view of mountain meadows. Yet it still wasn't particularly dark. Everything was plain and gray in this light. Let's just get on the bed, he said, and lie there for a while. Not that I want to dictate to you. But that's what I need to do. Is that pathetic?

She closed her bag, set it on the floor, and unbuckled her sandals, with her silver hair hanging. It unfurled, he thought, like a Möbius strip. What do you think? she asked.

New territory.

Maybe I should tell you something. Because love and death—I've been there, too.

Sure, he said. Break the ice.

Barefoot, she got on the bed. She sat up next to him with her back against the headboard and her hands pressed palm to palm against her skirt. While she talked, he lay with his forearms across his eyes, as if by negating the room he might see better, but actually this was a habit of his, something he did to live inside himself—lie down, cover his face—for hours at a time, at home, in the evenings, instead of watching TV or reading.

I grew up in farm country, she said, but that doesn't really describe it. Do you know where Odessa is? In eastern Washington? I grew up thirteen miles from Odessa, in what they call the Channeled Scablands. We grew wheat. It was really pretty simple. But let me back up a little. Do you know the Spokane Floods? I'm terrible on eras, but a long time ago there were the Spokane Floods. They took the country down to black rock—basalt. Except for these islands of good soil: the hills. So what got farmed were the fingers, the islands of soil—the benches and the feet of benches. Flying in from Minneapolis, you see it. The dark channels are the rock, and the yellow is soil, because our soil was loess, and loess looks yellow. Wind brings it. It's like dust, but it grows wheat. Dry-land wheat, no irrigating. My mother spent a lot of time battling with loess, and my father had farmer's lung, probably because of it. He coughed all the time. At night especially. We had seven thousand acres and a pile of combine parts. My dad was always worrying about weather. Everything was always touch and go, marginal, at the mercy—one more bad season and we'd have to go, but where? That was a topic of ongoing conversation. It's the bleakest of the bleak kind of farming, what you grow when nothing else will grow. Odessa—Odessa is Russian Mennonite. Actually German. Or, rather, German Russian—Germans who migrated to Russia but then came here. Isolationists. They want to do their own thing. They go in for the hardscrabble places like Odessa. We weren't Mennonite or Russian or German. We actually lived closer to a place called Lamona, but Lamona had nothing, so we went to Odessa. Lamona was a siding, a railroad siding. So I went to school in Odessa on a yellow bus. And the grocery store, but not the doctor. You needed a doctor, you drove to Spokane. When you were really going big, you went to Spokane. An hour and a half. We drove up to Davenport and went that way. Do you remember Expo? World's fair in Spokane? I worked at Expo in '74. I was twenty-two. But I'm ahead of myself. What year was it when I was sixteen? It was . . . '68. But I had no idea what was going on in the world. We were so out there, the only connection was *Time* magazine. At the little library in town, which was open two days a week and about the size of this room. Plus television, except we pulled in only one channel at our house, KREM, which was CBS. People say '68 was seminal, but Odessa? I remember hearing about a boy from Wilson Creek, not far from where I grew up, who got killed in Vietnam. . . . Sixty-eight, that was Martin Luther King, Bobby Kennedy. I mean, I heard about it. . . . Okay—you get my point.

With his forearms still across his eyes, he said, The tulies.

Anyway, there was this boy. He was just this boy I thought was handsome, nobody special, just one of the boys I went to school with, but he was older. Most of the boys there, they were farm boys, like this boy. Billy, Tommy, names like that. This boy was named Clifton Rider, and he was eighteen, and he lived closer to Harrington. Two years older. The bus I took to school would start picking up kids toward Harrington, and then it would come our way. So I would always see this Clifton Rider, and he would always be sitting way at the back with his brothers—he had two brothers. And their friends. Boys. We didn't—I mean, my sister and I—we didn't go back there, we sat toward the front with a group of girls. Our whole school was eighty, ninety kids. Everybody knew everybody. There weren't really cliques. The kids on the sports team were the kids in the school play; otherwise, there's no school play.

What about Clifton?

Clifton, too. He was okay. Not the star of anything, just . . . average, except for his looks. At least, I thought so.

Not a tall guy, not a boy like a lot of high-school boys, with a lot of body language—pretty quiet guy. Very down-to-earth. They grew wheat like we did, the Riders, but they had pota- toes and hay, too, or at least they did in '68. Sometimes we went for groceries to Harrington, because my parents knew the store owners there—my dad was in their Lions for some reason, the Harrington Lions instead of Odessa, prob- ably because of something petty—that area was petty. So we would see the Rider kids around there in Harrington. Clif- ton, the oldest. My sister and I never talked to them, but we knew who they were, and we knew their reputation, which is that they were Pentecostals, whereas just about everyone else around there was Lutheran. I shouldn't say that. There were also Congregationalists. And Seventh-day Adventists. But my family was Lutheran, pretty seriously Lutheran. We went to church every Sunday. Our pastor didn't push hard. The Pentecostals—people thought they were extremists. Just rumors, the things you'd think of—speaking in tongues, lay- ing on of hands. So the Riders, they were associated with that. One thing they did do, they had the dress code in their family. The Riders looked neat. Short haircuts, and they always had their shirts buttoned up and tucked in. All three of the boys were sort of bullish in appearance. Like their dad. Thick neck, wide face, heavy brow, even when they were just kids. Which can be, actually, more expressive than you think. I mean, when Clifton was up or down, you knew it.

She stopped. The lodge had recently been girded to earth- quake standards, but the windows still creaked when the wind blew. He heard that, and when she moved a little, he heard the bedsprings. The noise and the movement of the bed were considerable, so he peeped out from under his forearm. She was trying to get more support from the pillow at her back by pumping it like an accordion. Take mine, he said. I'm not using it.

No. This is fine. I'll just fluff it up a little.

She got settled again and went back to her story. Where was I? she asked. Probably on a tangent. All I'm really trying to say is that Clifton went out on a limb and talked to me. When we were getting off the bus at school. He was behind me in the aisle, and he said . . . I don't know. I could lie and say he said something great, but the truth is, I can't remember. But he said something. Then we got off the bus and walked together for, seriously, a fraction of a second. After that he said hi all the time. On the bus or elsewhere. Just hi. I said hi back, trying not to flush. I would turn red and sweat, though. This went on for a couple of weeks, during which I thought about Clifton obsessively. I was in love with Clifton Rider. It was really hard for me on the bus. Same thing at school. I couldn't concentrate. I told my sister I had a crush on Clifton, and she told everybody, and then a rumor came back that Clifton had a crush on me, too.

One day when he said hi to me at school, he caught me in a braver-than-usual mood, and I was able to say, "Hey, Clifton, hold up for a second. I want to ask you something. You've been hearing rumors. I've been hearing them, too. What have you heard? Rumors are always flying around here." He beat around the bush on that. He didn't want to answer straight on, directly. But the upside was, we'd gotten past hi, so now when we passed each other in the halls we would both roll our eyes to indict the lack of privacy at Odessa High School. We were locked in by it. We had something to share. The "This place is just too small" conversation kids have in small towns. You could go on from there. You could take it from there. We were at the friend stage now, but the whole time, I was in love. I wanted Clifton to . . . just . . . take me in his arms and kiss me or something. So far we're not even sitting together on the bus. Remember that? I couldn't decide if he was nervous or if he just didn't like me the way I liked him. Two years older was a different category. Maybe he liked me, maybe he didn't. Remember "Both Sides Now"? Sixty-eight? I just had to hear that song and—bang—even though it had nothing to do with me or Clifton. But that's music for you.

Ditto.

"Both Sides Now"?

It's possible to go there if your mood's right.

Her assenting murmur was not entirely firm, and made him think that covering his face while he spoke had gotten rude. He uncovered it and sat up. Did with his pillow what she'd done with hers. I like his name, he said. Clifton Rider.

Clifton, she answered. I thought it was great. And his last name, too. Super-cowboy!

You had a cowboy thing.

No. But I had a Clifton thing, so that smoothed the way for a cowboy thing—singular. Clifton was sort of cowboy in a neatnik way.

He rode a horse?

Actually, a dirt bike. Or a farm bike. They had a thing

in Odessa called Deutschesfest, and it included a motorcycle run. People screamed out of town and came back a couple hours later covered with dust. I don't know what it was all about. That's just what we did then. I was down there with my friends, probably just hanging around, doing nothing, laughing at the polka music outside the beer garden, and Clifton rolls up on his bike and says, Hey! Hop on! I didn't think. I just saddled up, figuring my friends would sort of chalk it up to the Deutschesfest spirit. A farm bike, that was how you got around—kids took these farm bikes into the Scablands. All the epic teen-ager stories were about bikes in the Scablands. People went for parties. There were places we knew about. You could get down over the base of a bench and be out of the wind where a lot of old fencing had been dumped and build a bonfire, and drink whatever. We used to pool our money and send someone to this place in Spokane, a little store that didn't card. But me and Clifton—we didn't do it, but we came close. Oh boy, Clifton! By a fencepost fire. Then we went back, because we had to. People would miss us. They'd all be talking. It was a huge concern. What if people knew? So we went back to Deutschesfest, and he let me off. I found my friends and said, "Yeah, great ride, we went out toward Duck Lake or something." I found my parents in the food tent and did, you know, sausage and strudel, but it was one of those "Aren't you hungry, somethin' wrong?" kind of dinners, because I was on Cloud Nine. Blissed out. Couldn't eat. Because of Clifton.

How do I explain this? I lost my virginity. But it was really tough for me and Clifton to get together, because my parents were not going to go for this guy. I had to hide him. Not that they paid attention. They thought exclusively about wheat, is what I thought then. They weren't human to me. Wheat on the brain. The farming game. But I told my sister, and she was good about things. We were close—still close. She lives in Denver. You know what? You always have to have an accomplice. When she fed the dogs at night, she muzzled them for me. That way, after my parents went to bed I could climb out the window and not set off barking. And get with Clifton. He'd be waiting by the shed with condoms in his pocket. He brought blankets, and he'd be standing there with the blankets, and, you know, we'd go into the shed. We'd go into a corner of the shed and wrap up in blankets. For hours. Sometimes until it was almost morning. Then Clifton would creep off into this little ravine where he'd stashed his bike out of earshot. I pulled the dog muzzles before I climbed back in. You have to wonder how many kids are doing this. Sneaking around. A lot, but only a few of them are having a great time, if they're honest, and those are the ones who are madly in love.

Maybe you've been there. Have you been there, Odessa? It's like Spokane. You look at the weather report for Spokane, it's at least low twenties just about every night after Thanksgiving. Inside the shed, maybe it's thirty-two. With the blankets and us, better than that. We whispered all the time, because we were scared. Whispered conversation. The natural subject when someone's eighteen is, What are you going to do with your life? Clifton didn't know. If he didn't get drafted, he was hoping to work on farm equipment. Or for a seed company. But he didn't want to farm, and he didn't want to leave the county. He didn't want to leave because of me, he said. If he left he couldn't see me, and that would kill him. Me! Year before, I'm no one to anyone; then I turn sixteen, go through physical changes, and now Clifton Rider can't live without me. I'm aware of that. But, still, it's genuine. Puppy love is real to the puppies—completely real. Hey—I went to Spokane with my parents and my sister every year to go Christmas shopping, and that year, I bought Clifton an album by The Doors. It was snowing, and there were cars off the road near the air-force base—Fairchild Air Force Base. I say this because it was a bad snow year. It piled up. Hard to say how much. Three feet, maybe? Never got warm enough to melt, either. Just kept adding, usually at night. A lot of mornings, we had fresh snow on the ground. When was this pattern going to stop? That kind of weather, notable weather—they had the roads plowed and sanded, but they couldn't keep up. People liked talking about the wipe-outs and near misses. Small town, no real news. The lights went on at our house—my mom liked Christmas lights. Snow's downtime for wheat farmers. My dad played with lights.

I've been guilty of that. When the kids were young. To make them happy.

And did Christmas lights make them happy?

I feel bad for my kids. That's the— Sorry.

We're here, she answered. The door's shut. We're here, and that's what we came for.

They took in their room. It was spartan at best. The money went to the lobby, not the rooms, and, in accordance with the mountain, there was a dearth of appointments. But she was right: they were here, whatever the appointments, and, anyway, he didn't care about appointments. So it was all right—maybe—to mention his kids. Clifton, he said. Clifton Rider.

The weather I described was bad for me and Clifton. Icy roads didn't exactly lend themselves to shed trysts. Too hard for Clifton to get around on his bike. Footsie under the table in the school lunchroom became it. My parents got wind—small town, of course—and my dad down-talked the Riders incessantly. He said he didn't know anything about them except that they were Holy Rollers and hunted without permission, out of season. Tongue speakers. Foot washers. Who'd they sell grain to? Who'd they buy fuel from? Where'd they get fertilizer? They didn't use the people my dad used, so they must be terrible human beings. My mom didn't cotton to the Riders, either. I was too young to have a boyfriend. I needed to be thinking about other things. Well: I put the emphasis on *friend* whenever Clifton came up. But my sister knew everything.

So. I told Clifton I had a Christmas present wrapped up for him and ready to go. But snow kept falling all through December. Clifton wrote me love notes. Clifton, with his dirty, greasy farm bike—Clifton wrote love notes. How he thought about me constantly. Sweet little amorous folded-up notes. I'm not saying Clifton was a poet, but his notes were good. You wouldn't think that was the case. Thick-necked farm boy. I really liked this about him—underneath, the note writer. Just me, no one else ever saw the real Clifton. Actually, I didn't get to see him much, either, because of the snow that December. Our notes were about, how could we get together? Then—winter vacation, or Christmas vacation, so now I'm not even seeing him at school. It's literally physically painful not to see someone when you're that much in love. Finally, not Christmas Eve but the day before Christmas Eve, Clifton tells his parents he's going duck hunting. He borrows his dad's fake ducks—decoys, they're called—and stuffs them in sacks and ties them to his farm bike. Gets out the gun, goes through all the motions. Gets out the waders, the duck call, the Elmer Fudd cap—all the duck-hunting accoutrement clichés. All so he can rev up at three a.m. without his parents' wondering why.

Guy got to me in a snowstorm. Came in through the back field so the dogs wouldn't get wind of him. I woke up because snowballs were hitting my window. There's Clifton in the Elmer Fudd cap. I opened up and told him to be quiet—you know, a finger to my mouth, shush. It's snowing, but the moon is out. Clifton is brushing snow off his shoulders. Stuff is falling hard, which is good, because it'll cover his tracks—maybe he hadn't thought of that. Maybe he wasn't as smart as I thought he was. Or maybe he was. I don't know. But, anyway, I sent him to the shed. I pointed at the shed, he went, I got dressed—two sweaters, best shoes I had in the room—but then, with the snow, it didn't seem like I could get out the window. Too slippery. Too dangerous. I tried, but it couldn't be done. I was going to have to tiptoe down the stairs, which meant getting past my parents' bedroom without waking them up. Impossible. My mom was a light sleeper, lifelong insomniac. I didn't know what to do. What could I do? I looked for Clifton, but Clifton was in the shed. I was stuck—snowbound, as they say, on the one hand, parent-bound on the other. No getting out.

No answer. I kept looking out the window. I thought that, after a while, Clifton would come see what was up and I could explain it to him, my predicament. But he didn't. So I just went on wondering what to do. Finally, I went down the hall and said, "I can't sleep. There's a lot of new snow. I'm gonna go outside for a few minutes." That seemed innocent enough. And it got me past them with the Doors album and out the door, and then I ran to the shed. But no Clifton. No Clifton in the shed. I'd say it was probably about five degrees outside, and fifteen in the shed. Clifton'd left me a note, and while I don't have it memorized word for word, it was basically to the effect of, "What happened? I waited. I love you. I miss you. I need you. Let's get married so we can stop sneaking around like this." And he'd left me a little Christmas present, nicely wrapped, which I put in my coat pocket and didn't open right away, because I had other things to think about, other things to be nervous about. I went out, and I could see his boot prints going off across the back field. Filling in fast. It's still dark, but now I'm thinking when my dad gets up he's going to see those prints and know. So I walk out a ways, until that's taken care of, his prints are blurred by mine, and a few times, when I'm far enough from the house, I call for Clifton. Real loud, but lost in the snow. Then I have to turn back. I'm frozen to the bone. I can phone him later and explain what happened. Give me the benefit of the doubt and let me be a little romantic here—it was very poetic. Sixteen, out there in the snow, in love, pining, and calling Clifton's name one more time before turning back. I can still hear my voice not traveling.

Go ahead. I don't begrudge you the right to . . . Just go ahead.

That's because of your own life, she said. That's what I saw the first time we met. At that wine bar.

She touched his temple. Stroked his hair—what was left of his hair. You know what? she said. I look right through you and see the boy inside. Boy Clifton's age. I mean, I can look right through you now and see you.

I do that. But come on—what happened?

Terrible, she said. I hate small towns. Anyway, the phone. You know, the dreaded phone call. My dad took it—"Bad news," he told me. "Sit down for this. That 'friend' of yours, Clifton Rider? They found him this morning. On Mohler Road. Skid-out accident, broke his leg, froze. Poor kid. I hope you're gonna be okay. You okay? That's a hard thing to get over when a teen dies. I—"

Clifton died?

Died.

And he wanted to marry you.

He said that, anyway. His gift was a ring. A band from Spokane. An engagement ring.

She paused on that, and so did he, because he didn't know what to say in the face of it. After all, she'd more than implied that she believed in love as something greater than adolescent hormones. Although, again, maybe that was wrong. Maybe her point was: kids are so dumb that at sixteen she would have married Clifton Rider, which would have meant passing her life in Odessa, or near Odessa, coughing up loess, watching the price of wheat, eating Deutschesfest strudel, and making sure her kids never sneaked around behind her back having premarital sex. Hmmm, he said. So which Doors album did you get him?

Waiting for the Sun.

She went silent again, and then reached for her toes—he had the feeling so as to hide her face from him.

Hey, he said.

But still she spoke with her head down: The big song was "Hello, I Love You," but I don't know. Not so great. The one I listened to after Clifton died was "Not to Touch the Earth." Jesus, that song! He loved that song. Clifton liked Jim Morrison, the Dionysian poet.

She still wouldn't look at him. Why was that? Once more that silver hair of hers spiraled down like a Möbius strip. Okay, he said. Let me get my phone. Let me see if I can get it on my phone. He got up, found his phone, dropped, dragged, and brought up The Doors, "Not to Touch the Earth." Are you ready? he asked. I've got it here.

No.

You don't want to hear it?

Okay. Go.

Somewhat banal—"Not to touch the earth, Not to see the sun, Nothing left to do, but Run, run, run"—and, when not banal, cryptic in the ecstatic Morrison vein. But did it matter? Because now the new woman in his life was crying. She was crying hard enough to make him see approximately where he stood in her life. A trip to Paradise with a guy met on match .com. It had come to that. They were doing their best. He touched her fingers and she took his hand. Who was this person he was about to make love with? Or was that the right term—making love?

Tenant

He was sitting down to dinner when the finder called. If you wanted to call it dinner. Two scrambled eggs and toast with peanut butter, which he planned to eat in front of the television. He'd plated his food and poured his beer, he was just now pulling the ottoman close and trying to recall where he'd left the remote—there it was between the picks for his gums a dental hygienist had given him that morning and some Sunday-paper advertising circulars; probably he'd have to slap it a little because the batteries inside were loose. Should he answer or let his machine take the call? The eggs were warm, the beer was cold. He was ready to eat; he didn't need a hassle. Answering the phone would mean a physical effort. He walked the six steps, though, to the caller-ID box, and when it registered with him that the caller was his finder, he put down the beer and picked up. "Yes," he said.

This finder—he hardly knew him—liked pleasantries before business. This finder was from the school of socially correct throat-clearing and so, in a tone of droll commiseration, described the current weather—miserable, rainy—and the terrible traffic on Interstate 90 from Mercer Island to the 405 interchange. According to him there were two good options—well-qualified people who checked out on every front—as a result of his professional efforts. He'd shown the apartment three times that afternoon, first to a woman who admired the remodel—the great-room space, the light, the cork floors—but who didn't want to move from her apartment down the corridor: "A voyeur," said the finder. "Someone just looking." Then to a nurse who wanted eagerly to rent it—a woman who "would make a perfectly good renter." Then to a woman who was the broker's top pick because of her references and "an off-the-charts credit score somewhere in the low-mid-eight-hundreds."

"Go with your top pick," he told the finder.

The finder arranged matters. The renter, whose name was Williams, Lydia Williams, signed the Lease/Rental Agreement and initialed each page. Her signature was indecipherable—as it was on her check for the first and the last months' rent and a prorated eleven days, and on her check for the damage deposit—but her initials were, by contrast, stark and plain. Lydia Williams, renter, he thought, of a modest two-bedroom apartment with a garage. Lydia Williams, cryptic nonpresence, intangible so far because he hadn't seen her, but generator—he hoped faithfully and smoothly—of perpetual rental income. He put a copy of their agreement in his "Apartment" file, along with her application and credit report, but not before confirming that it accurately portrayed their payment arrangement, namely, that Lydia Williams' rent would henceforth flow from her bank account to his via electronic transfer on the fifteenth of each month; the fifteenth for tax purposes—he liked it for its symmetry. He also filed a letter from the finder, who therein reported providing Williams with two sets of keys to the front door, garage, mailbox, and garbage/recycling enclosure, and explaining parking regulations to her, and parceling out to her the right decal for her windshield and the right pass for her guests, and stressing to her the rules in force at the Blue Vista Condominium Complex, and leading her on a "walk-through" so she could list flaws she wouldn't be responsible for at move-out. But she'd listed nothing, either because she didn't want to or hadn't looked closely, or maybe because he'd worked so diligently to render the apartment rentable, to put it in good order. He'd painted the inside of the front door, patched the drywall. There were new batteries in the smoke detectors.

Lydia Williams—as the finder put it in his final report before siphoning off his outlandish fee—moved in without a hitch. Invisible, an abstraction, RENTER—all caps—but indeed her rent got paid, expediently and electronically, on the fifteenth of month two, and with no trouble, no communication. It was as if Lydia Williams remained in the finder's hands—she existed contractually but not in person; he could not have said what she looked like or how she sounded; now and again he stopped to wonder who Lydia Williams was, but his questions about her had to do with her reliability as a rent payer and with whether she could change a lightbulb in figurative terms, i.e., whether she could save him time and money, by virtue of solid do-it-yourself skills, on repairs and maintenance. He wondered but made no move to find out about her, fearing that by asserting himself he might pave the way for a burdensome relationship, invite nuisance, regret his forwardness, ultimately end up with more trouble, work, and concern than if he'd stayed in the background.

Finally, he sent her a benign and innocent enough e-mail. Or rather forwarded an attachment from the secretary of the Blue Vista Homeowners' Association about mandatory chimney inspections; to this he added "FYI" and his initials. Nothing in reply from Lydia Williams, not even terse and perfunctory acknowledgment, no thank you for forwarding—maybe she didn't get it? Should he re-send? No. He did nothing instead. He didn't want to seem in any way, shape, or form urgent—the opposite; he wanted to seem distant. Yet here he'd closed in on her with the necessary-chimney-inspection message. From behind some pretty solid layers of safeguard, true, but he'd communicated with—with whom? Was there someone on the other end? Another electronic transfer of rent money went smoothly, weeks passed, and then, goaded from within and by something he lacked a name for, he sent her a second communiqué in the form of an attachment—BVHA-provided information on "Smart Preparations for Power Outages"—once more with "FYI" and his initials, timing this safely purposeful missive to coincide with televised meteorological angst about an imminent snowstorm. Then the storm came, like vindication, or like justification. Because he'd only done what a landlord should do, correct?

Normally in the course of a day, normally in the mid-afternoon, the bluest hours, when life felt—there was no right word—he would set out in his car to perform errands—plus on Saturdays make a good-son visit to his parents—but that was impossible given this crisis of bad weather: snow piling up through pallid hours. He stayed inside, looking out the window regularly to take the measure of the snow and monitoring television coverage of it. Midafternoon, his disheartening time, came, and lower temperatures to boot. He tried to nap—lay down, half slept—but sometimes it was the case, strangely enough, that lying down made his right-leg sciatica more buzzy. It did this time. He got up, checked the thermostat, sat in a Windsor chair—one with arms and a fairly plump cushion—and read *The Week* in a vexed state, then did something he often felt tempted to do but tried to control because it only made his sullenness worse: online investment research. And now that he was, against his better judgment, online—he was online too much—should he contact his new tenant? The sense of rigor he depended on to keep from making social errors was eroded and finally sufficiently compromised by a day without errands, and by the pressure of feeling snowbound, to warrant what, exactly? Writing her an e-mail. He wrote one nervously. Subject heading, "WATER TURN OFF." Now the hard part. Dear Tenant? Hi Lydia Williams? Eventually he thought of a clever expedient. Once again he wrote "FYI" and his initials. The rest he sent attached, as if, by extrapolation from his prior communiqués, she should assume it was from the secretary of the BVHA instead of from him—a strategy of minor but not innocent misdirection—to wit, "A reminder that if you are going to be away for an extended period of time, please turn off your main water valve. And it wouldn't hurt to let one of your neighbors know how to reach you just in case there is a need to enter—you know, like for frozen pipes that burst and create havoc."

Conceivably this might just prompt Lydia Williams to divulge personal information—when she would be away, where she was going—though that was jumping the gun, he knew; there was no reason to believe she was about to take a trip. But if, for example, she was driving for the holidays to a hamlet in Montana, well then, this ruse would give him search fodder: he could try "Lydia Williams Cut Bank" and see what happened. Maybe answer the question "Is that where she's from?" Cut Bank or another hypothetical destination? Because so far his surf stalking had yielded about a goose egg; there were just too many Lydia Williamses; even when he'd plugged in her rental-application data, he'd come up with pretty much zilch. Yes, "WATER TURN OFF" was a foray with an invasive secondary intention. Who knew where it might lead? Maybe they would end up discussing this matter of his entering her/his—it was still his—apartment in the case of burst pipes and havoc. The point was, he could be turning a corner with this potential new e-mail. Nerve-racking. And then he hit on an even better stratagem. He wrote, after "FYI" but before his initials, "The main water valve is hidden behind the upper right corner of the washing machine." Could he bring himself to click Send on that? It would be personal—outside of an attachment.

Poised over his trackpad, he looked out the window, where a very small bird was having difficulty finding a perch that was not too cold—it kept fluttering around in a snarl of small branches, raising puffs of powder. Not the kind of thing he took an interest in—nature. But right now, entertaining in its wintry, desperate way. Should he click on Send? He should not click on Send. He highlighted and deleted "The main water valve is hidden behind the upper right corner of the washing machine," but sent the attachment ostensibly from the secretary of the BVHA along with "FYI" and his initials. So no change in status. Safe.

She e-mailed back almost immediately with: "Hi. In case I need it—where's the valve? Thanks—Lydia." To which he replied, "Behind the upper right corner of the washing machine." No initials.

There followed this exchange: "I don't see it. L." "It's a little bit hidden, but it's there. S." "I still don't see it." "It's a gate valve—red. Three feet or so off the ground. Right corner." "Not there that I can tell." "I am happy to come by the apartment on a day and at a time of your convenience so as to chase this down." "You don't need to do that." "I have errands to do anyway." "I'm here this coming Saturday morning." "What about ten?" "See you at 10 on Saturday. L." "Weather permitting. Roads being open." "Maybe between now and then I'll find it." "Right back corner. Let me know."

Saturday arrived. The temperature was much improved, the snow had melted almost entirely from the main roads— dirty water roiling toward drains—and sufficiently from side roads to allow for safe driving; there would be no excuse along the lines of weather; he must go as promised to visit his parents but first to the Blue Vista. So be it. What did they say—what was the expression? The saying, he remembered, was "Time to man up." He took along his faithful road companions—a stainless-steel travel mug filled with Earl Grey tea, his glasses, their case, a fine lens cloth, and a spray bottle of lens cleaner—but decided, this morning, not to listen to his radio; he needed to think; what would he say? He would say, Hello, I'm sorry you've had trouble locating the valve, it's good to finally meet you, where did the time go, excuse me for failing to introduce myself earlier, I don't want to be remiss or derelict in my duties as a landlord so if there's anything you need, some way I can help you, please don't hesitate to e-mail, text, or call, did I put both my home number and cell in the rental agreement, you might have one but not the other. Have both now. I'm at your disposal, of course, when it comes to maintenance, repairs, and questions about the condominium complex or about your apartment and garage, and also, before long it will be time for me to come through and lightly sand and then re-oil the butcher-block counter, the process is intrusive, I know, but necessary unfortunately, because otherwise unsanitary food stains work their way into the wood and then you have to sand even more deeply to get them out again, plus proliferating mold; better to sand and oil on a regular basis, about every four months although the intervals lengthen as you build up a bit of a surface and get ahead. And while I'm there, every four months, I check the lint trap and maybe do a few other things, just make sure the drains are clear in the bathtub, shower, and sinks, one matter I've been meaning to talk to you about and that is that under the kitchen sink the plumbing is fragile, this is the name of the game these days—cheap materials—so it just helps to be a little bit delicate under there, not move things around too much and therefore cause the pipes to rotate, or they eventually loosen and a drip starts; all of the pieces in that system relate to one another, so when you tighten one you loosen its neighbor, by which I mean the adjoining coupled piece; it can be frustrating; the next time we—you, or me—have or has a problem with those pipes I'm going to bite the bullet and just go ahead and replace everything with stainless steel and that should be the end of it, I can't tell you how many times leaks from under the kitchen sink have caused the cork flooring to warp and buckle, cork was such an unfortunate choice for wet areas and it's a mistake I'll never make again—in this manner he got to the Blue Vista parking lot, where slush and debris—fallen branches, old snow—were heaped in his appointed slot. A pile of wet dross and slop was in the way, storm detritus, wrack and wreckage of the sort that might exacerbate depression.

He knocked on her door at 10:01. At last: Lydia Williams.

Later—opening a little journal he kept sporadically—whole months were missing—where to start? With her or with what she'd done with his apartment? With her, of course, Lydia Williams, five foot five approximately, 115 or 120 pounds, age in the range of thirty-five to forty, black hair in a crocheted beanie skull cap, eyes about halfway between hazel and auburn but, a moment later, closer to green—he thought maybe green on the eerie order of honeydew-melon flesh when she moved to her right so he could cross the threshold while they maintained the right culturally ordained distance. Dressed like, it was impossible to say, just that she was wearing baggy drab sweatpants underneath this, was it called a shirtdress? With buttons down the front. And a bold leather belt that drew it together in—he was taking a chance here using this word because he had so little clothing terminology—was it pleats? And down booties with hard soles. What was her look? Did it have a name? Mix and match? Potluck medley? Vintage anarchic? Intentional clash? She made him think of politically activated peasants from the era of Tolstoy—minus the tall boots—in this case a Tolstoyan with an air of only partial political zeal, a comrade with some poetry and whimsy and those parts of her stronger than her politics; either all of that or Maid Marian dressed for bow pulling. Lydia Williams was a little bit pale, not on the side of faded or blanched, not along the lines of ghostly and wan, more sort of north of Irish, or south of Icelandic, but maybe this vagrant ethereality of hers was just a trick of his canned lighting scheme coupled with the snaring of her hair in that clingy beanie, leaving a considerable forehead tract to catch not just the forty-watt recessed halogens but also what still seemed, to him, like snow light coming through the windows, even though snow was, for the most part, past. The staying-in look—the staying in on Saturday a.m. to drink tea and read look, not PJs and a robe but not going-out clothes; he added to this rapid, first-impression assessment her "natural" approach when it came to makeup, she had something or other on, he didn't know what to call it, but not very much of it, almost none, still, her skin had a layer of something or other which was meant to, he thought now, deepen her paleness, probably a contradiction in terms when he thought about it—a deeper paleness? The point was, after getting up this morning she'd put something on, the better to greet him, maybe feeling that without it, what—but now that they'd passed along the short entry hall and into the great room he wasn't sure any longer; maybe she wore no makeup at all; light changed everything; in the great room, even though the light was cleaner and more telling, he decided Lydia Williams could be under thirty-five; after all, a cold, full, and naked light didn't reveal more forehead furrows, laugh lines, crow's feet, or other signatures of late-thirtysomething aging, no, she didn't have as many time-related skin flaws as he'd guessed, fleetingly, would be revealed here when, a few seconds before, he'd made some initial but not perfunctory observations about her in the less well-lit foyer. Though he hardly had time to think about that now, overwhelmed as he was by her style of apartment decorating/furnishing in all its density, color, texture, and vivacity—he didn't recognize the great room; was this really his apartment? It looked like a curio shop and an import emporium—a phantasmagoria or multicultural souk—paper lanterns, prayer flags, tapering vases, wicker baskets, lucky cats, mounded throw pillows, whatnots, gewgaws, knickknacks, tchotchkes, a naked mannequin, a sombrero, some gourds, a divan on wheels, strings of twinkling Christmas lights, it was all too much to take in with any depth in the context of this, his introductory visit, there were just so many horizontal and vertical planes of product and incident—streamers, pendants, hung crystals, strung beads—though it did occur to him to wonder how everything was attached, fixed, arrayed, pinned, to what extent his perfect surfaces were now compromised by tacks, tape, stains, and picture hooks, how much work it might be one day to repair this gaudy and shimmering bazaar, to put things back to how they'd been before—clean, unmarred, easy to maintain, four white walls and a ceiling. Plus the cork floor. A landlordish consideration—the sort of thing he had to think about. For example, these very large portraits on the most proximate, the east, wall, framed and hung—he hoped the drywall could handle them without fissuring. They were all of multi-armed goddesses derived from Hindu mythology, including Kali, blue and bloodthirsty, stepping as she was on the throat of a dead man and wearing as she was a belt of severed heads; this he would have liked to look at more closely—a girdle of amputated arms, a necklace of skulls, some cobras, some she-demons, a sickle, a sword—but right now, the thing was—Lydia Williams. Lydia Williams and the question between them of the apparently missing, or at least hard to find, water shut-off valve. Time to come to that. Especially because, throughout his observations—both of her and her created world—they'd been engaged in dialogue. She'd said—at the door—"Hi," he'd answered, "Can I come in?," there'd been the few short steps between the foyer and the great room during which he'd thought of the terms "shirtdress" and "pleats," they'd reached the great room, she'd turned back toward him—a little ripple of the sub-belt, or was it midriff, "shirtdress" fabric—at which point he'd said, "The mysterious water valve," this prompting from Lydia Williams no smile or laughter, as he'd thought it might—it sounded wry in his ear—but instead just the words "I'm Lydia." "Shawn." "Sorry you had to come here." "I had to go to the store today anyway." "Where do you shop?" "Different places." "That's Kali. You probably know that. That one's Green Tara, the giver of prosperity." "How are things working out for you here?" "Perfect." "You like the apartment." "I love the apartment." "You're the first renter I've had here, you know. Before you, I lived here myself." "Where are you now?" "In a different place." At which point he felt it had gone too far in the direction of intimacy. Not landlordly. So he didn't tell her—he held back—about his parents' moving out of their house—the house he'd grown up in, in Shoreline, two blocks from Interstate 5—and into an apartment, or his return to the house of his childhood—paid for but a terrible maintenance miasma—or that he owned two other apartments, both in this complex, with reliable, long-term renters installed, both male, who rarely bothered him about anything—that he was Mr. Modest Landlord and Mr. Good Son. "Well," he said instead. "The water valve. I'll let you lead." All business.

She led the way to the guest bath/laundry center with its washer and dryer side by side on a counter at eye level— as opposed to stacked—which he explained to her now: "When I did the remodel I had every intention of stacking the machines—they were made to be stacked—but then it occurred to me there was a better way, something I could do to make the laundry work easier, that is, put them side by side, that way no one would have to bend over to load or empty the lower-level machine. Option A was stacked machines with a full-size water heater upright in an adjoining closet; option B was two small in-line water heaters down below behind slid-ing doors—see?—and side-by-side machines above. Obvi-ously I went with option B, but that's just me, not everyone would choose to do it that way." "Oh," she answered. "Okay." Not good.

Since the guest-bath/laundry-center foot-traffic area was limited, she stood outside its door—culturally correct bodily-distance protocol—while he stood in front of the side-by-side machines; this room was toned down but for a few touches probably meant to blend it into the loud great-room scheme—incense burner, candelabra, beaten copper bowl of scented potpourri, a fringy or tasseled shroud of paisley tapestry hung above the mirror—maybe it was an old shawl converted to this purpose. With no further ado, he went to work. "I'm just going to jimmy this machine back and forth a little to bring it out and create some space between it and the wall, but not too much, because I don't want to overstretch or put pressure on the hot and cold water lines, causing them to leak; they're old-style rubber, thin walled and with a limited service life; I haven't replaced them yet with new and better, updated lines; there are washing-machine supply lines now made of braided stainless steel with a PVC core—really good, super-strong, with brass hex nuts and a fifteen-hundred-psi burst strength." He started his jimmying; he walked the machine out about nine inches; the front feet were now hanging off the coun-ter; the machine had tilted just a little, but not enough so that a dime placed on top—even without lint-crusted soap stains in the way—would slide off onto the unfortunate and falsely-advertised-as-water-resistant cork flooring panels. "Now I need a chair," he said, "so I can climb up there, look over the top, and locate that ever-mysterious water shut-off valve whose location it's dire to ascertain in case of emergency." Again he meant to make a little joke, this one via incongruous language; again Lydia Williams did not take his bait; they were of slightly different generations; his hair was gray at the temples and some new sensibility of humor was in play that he wasn't party to; he'd been left behind at forty-six. "I actually have a stepladder," she said. "Would you want that instead of a chair?" "Either's fine." "I'll grab the stepladder." "Okay. I'll wait here." She took a half-step inside and seemed to mull, squeezing her chin between her left thumb and forefinger. "I think the stepladder might fit a little better," she said. The beanie snaring her hair had slid a little to the left, so that the darkly netted chaos or the bird's nest of her tresses was no longer on top but on the side, beside her neck, and something else—available to his eye now given the fluorescent light of the guest bath/laundry center—she had a few light freckles, a little umber mottling, that complemented her communist-cell peasant/artist look, or maybe it was a hip volunteer soup-line ladler in a hairnet look, a ladler with a social conscience who had retained artistic flair.

She went for the ladder. This gave him time to notice that the toilet bowl had one of those blue deodorizers in it—good—and that beside the incense burner was a packet of Pondicherry frankincense cones. With one hand he kept a little pressure on the tipped washing machine, lest it decide of its own accord to fall over—that would be a real disaster, potentially injurious to him or to the toilet bowl—with the other he picked up the Pondicherry packet and read its promotional and informational material—made at Sri Aurobindo Ashram . . . hand-mixed . . . friendly to the environment . . . packed in wood-free cotton and banana pulp hand-made paper . . . he could hear Lydia Williams returning with the stepladder—the padding of her down booties across the cork floor—so he put the incense packet back and just stood there as if—for her benefit—he was content to do nothing but hold up the machine. "Great," he said, when she showed him the stepladder and began unfolding it. "A three-step kitchen model. That looks like a good one." "Be careful, though. Don't get hurt." "I'm always careful. Safety first." "I did what you're doing. But I didn't see the valve." "You pulled the machine out?" "No, but I used the ladder." "I probably should have told you to pull the machine out." "I got a pretty good look. I even used a flashlight." "The deep, abiding mystery of the water valve," he said. This time, finally, she smiled: he'd worn her down.

He took the ladder. "You're sure you're okay?" she said. "I'm okay." "It's just that you have to climb the ladder and keep the machine from tipping any further now that its front is off of the counter. That's two things at once." "I think I can do it, though." "Maybe I should help." "Tight quarters here." "Yes, but, like this"—she came in, braced herself against the drop-in sink console, and pressed her right hand—bulbous finger pads, he noticed—strongly into the face of the slightly tilted washing machine— "I can hold it in place while you climb up and take a look." "You don't mind?" "No. It's fine."

"Well, if you don't mind then, thank you, that's helpful."
Whereas actually he was thinking that suddenly the two of
them were jammed into this little room together and that
the culturally correct distance protocol had been abrogated to
the point where he thought he could smell her hair inside its
beanie skull cap; after all, having risen already to step two of
her ladder, he was above her now; the closest part of her to
his nose was her hair; on the other hand, she would be aware,
potentially, of the smells emanating from the nether portions
of his body—what would that be like for her? Most people
have little awareness of their own smells, this was something
he knew because of a cousin who due to his restaurant work
often smelled like cumin but didn't know it; clothing heavily impregnated or infused with sweat and spice was not an
impression he wanted to make right now, so how fortunate that
this room was in his favor due to its hygienic blue-deodorizer
scent and verdure of concealing Pondicherry frankincense.
Something else: generally he was too slothful and depressed
to do laundry, but by a stroke of fortune—or due to exploi-
tation of a snowbound, errandless, in-home window of late
Wednesday morning domestic energy—his clothes were right
now washed, happily so given the rarity of current circumstance: proximity to a woman of child-bearing age; for that
matter, proximity to anybody. And yet, rising to the third and
final ladder step, he lacked confidence in his odors. It seemed
to him he had to be—surely he was—an olfactory offense to
Lydia Williams, and probably an offense in his other particu-
lars. How could this not be the case?

Now he bent across the machine, draped himself over it

and looked down its back side. There were dust and cobwebs, there were hot and cold water lines, there was a power cord, but—no shut-off valve. "You're right," he said. "Huh." "Come down now," she answered. "The machine might fall over."

Failure. Failure at the moment of expected triumph. Abysmal, and proof of his worthlessness.

He came down, she took the ladder away, he walked the machine back into place, by the time he was done she was back and he said, "Do you mind if I wash my hands?" "No." And she gave him privacy to do it—she fled to the great room. Afterward he folded her hand towel to perfection. Then he came out and, standing beside her mannequin, said, "What's wrong with me? Suddenly I remember where it is." He went back and drew open the left-hand sliding door providing access to the dual-water-tank compartment. "Duh," he said. "Shut-off valve. Stupid. I can't believe it. Dumb. Moved it when I remodeled—there it is. Duh." "Great!" "God, I'm stupid." "Mystery solved—all's well that ends well."

He knew what that was—that was a dismissal. *Adiós, amigo, Auf Wiedersehen,* fool. Their business was done; she wanted him to go; he would not get a deeper, more thorough look at Kali, or for that matter, at any of the other goddesses on her wall. "All's well that ends well"—meaning, the end. He would leave and she would straighten the hair inside her beanie, reinforce her makeup scheme—if there was one—remove the sweatpants, down booties, and shirtdress, and replace them with things outdoorsy, warm, and casual, find her reusable shopping bags, and go outside with a scarf around her neck and her phone on to join her peers at the winter farmers' market with its displays of expensive cheeses and organic nuts—all this while he went to visit his parents in New Holly, where they lived not far from the light-rail line and in walking distance of a place that sold chapatis because his mother no longer cared to make her own, plus—he'd counted—their neighborhood had six pho shops. "All's well that ends well," except, first, she wanted to know about his last name, Ghemawat, which, she said, she'd seen on the rental agreement—and which she now mispronounced. Was that her fault? Why set her straight? Why do anything? The whole thing was impossible. "From India," he explained—meaning the name, not him, but certainly his answer could be taken to mean him—even though he'd been born three-quarters of a mile from where they stood right now and had never lived anywhere else, just Seattle. "Indian," he told the fair-skinned Lydia Williams, without knowing exactly what that meant about himself, or to what extent it was true, and feeling it was something he couldn't explain anyway, nor did he want to explain it. Besides, it was time to let this tenant live her life, time to leave so she could get on with her Saturday. It would be wrong of him to stay another minute. Sure, he owned the place, but what difference did that make? The two of them had no more business together. "I'm going to get out of your way now," he said. "Thank you," answered Lydia Williams.

Pilanesberg

They turned onto the R510. Every town they passed through had plentiful "rubbish," as his sister called it—barbed-wire compounds, and slovenly industry. His sister was a nerve-racking driver, not because she wasn't careful but because she was too careful, forcing other travelers to use the oncoming lane to make high-speed passes. They were on a road with no shoulders and crazy truckers; the "veldt"—another of his sister's terms—looked increasingly dramatic as they got farther from Johannesburg. Twice his sister stopped to use restrooms. Twice she took pills. Her hands trembled on the steering wheel.

They reached Pilanesberg—the Manyane Gate. She'd made a reservation at the Golden Leopard for a thatched-roof chalet that looked, to him, from the outside, better suited to the Lake District, but with a private patio and a barbecue on a stanchion that his sister called a *braai*. Inside, their quarters were air-conditioned. He was still jet-lagged; she was "away from death," as she put it, and wanted, for now, to take in the peace and do nothing, not go anywhere, not move, just rest. Besides, there would be better animal viewing as dusk approached—near dusk was when the animals came out. And so, settled in wicker chairs, they lingered in the cool chalet, talking about his photography and her cancer, and what he wanted to know, given that it was summer in South Africa and therefore hot outside: was the wig uncomfortable? It was okay with him if she took it off.

She took it off. Her skull was pitted. She'd packed her "boot" with food in coolers and bags—fruit, crackers, nuts, carrots, pomegranate juice, bread, a roasted chicken—all for him, because she couldn't eat anything. Around three, she looked at her watch and said that she was excited about animal viewing, though at Pilanesberg the chances of a Big Five experience—lion, leopard, rhino, elephant, and buffalo—were not as good as at Kruger. The ever-promising thing about Pilanesberg, she told him, was that it was transitional, somewhere in between dry and wet and thus eclectic in flora and fauna; further, because it was close to Johannesburg, it had been aggressively managed, and stocked via a program of translocation called Operation Genesis. Should they go take a look now? Maybe it was time to go. Especially if he wanted to take pictures; the light was good.

They went. The guard in uniform at Manyane Gate waved them through and, almost immediately, after rounding a bend, they saw zebras on a hillside. Not long after it was wildebeest, then rhinos at a mudhole, then a hardworking dung beetle in the road, small, pushing a big ball of dung. He took a photo of the dung beetle and thanked his sister for bringing him here. His sister, in the manner of a tour guide, told him that, for all of Pilanesberg's glories, it had challenges and problems because it was surrounded by a fence and reclaimed from land that had been farmed and grazed. Here was one indicative difficulty: the male elephants of Pilanesberg had been culled from a herd at Kruger and were apparently psychotic, having survived a population-control killing operation that had stressed them beyond the breaking point. This was why they were busy, in their new home, raping white rhinos and goring them to death with their tusks. Another example: there was a lion in the park—a rogue, bad, a lone hunter, crazy—who serially killed lionesses averse to his advances and then, repeatedly, copulated with their dead bodies. Was it Pilanesberg that caused this, since, in effect, it was unnatural, a massive zoo?

They came to a place where there were a lot of elephants, and because of that, a lot of Land Rovers and safari vehicles of the sort he was familiar with from television—open-air four-wheeling one-ton trucks with canvas tops and bolstered bumpers, driven by guides in ranger uniforms, and seated behind them, or standing up, passengers viewing the Pilanesberg elephants through binoculars and camera lenses. The herd milled on a plain of acacias, and as he and his sister idled in her car, elephants moved in front and behind, left and right, slowly, unconcerned, while all around the diesel engines of safari vehicles were shut off, the better to hear the noises elephants made—snorting, trammeling, trumpeting, thumping—as they cracked branches, ate grass, forced their way through brush, and dusted themselves. It was so arresting, so much what they'd come for, that they stayed for a long time, watching elephants and talking, while he took pictures. And then, since it was beginning to get dark, they drove toward the Manyane Gate.

The gate was closed. They idled in front of it with the entirely reasonable expectation that it would open automatically in the next moment and let them through, but nothing happened for such a long time that eventually they got out and stood in the headlights, talking about what to do next. It's widely known, he had been told, that, one, darkness falls quickly in Africa, and two, that African darkness seems exceptionally dark to foreign tourists. Already, at Manyane, it was dark in this way, except for the headlights, the stars, and a light on in the squat, modest guardhouse on the other side of the gate. "This is upsetting," his sister said. "The gate won't open."

The guard finally emerged from the guardhouse, walked toward them, put his hands on the gate, and explained to them that Manyane, like all the gates in the park, closed at 7 p.m., and that it was now—he looked at his watch—7:04 p.m.

What were they to do? His sister pressed the guard about this. "Obviously you have a key," she said, "so go get it and open the gate."

The guard pulled on the trouser fabric at his thigh, raised his leg, and set his boot on the gate's bottom rail. He grimaced and shook his head—no. He was a young black man, polite, apologetic, in a clean and pressed uniform and with a pistol on his hip, speaking in a quiet tone: "No, but I don't have a key," he said. "I have no key." He shrugged.

"No key," said his sister. "Okay, I get it." She went to her car, which was idling still, retrieved her handbag, and brought it to the gate. In the headlights again, she opened her wallet, removed some bills, and held them where the guard could take them through the bars. Her hand was shaking. "What's your name?" she said.

"Nelson."

"Well, Nelson," said his sister, "this is wrong of you, what you're doing here, you know. You have to open the gate right now. You don't have a choice—you have to open the gate. You can't just trap people in the park indefinitely. Come on now, Nelson, open the gate." She shook the money enticingly.

Nelson shrugged again and kept his distance from the bills. "It's true, truly, I have no key," he said. "There is no way for me to open the gate. Seven o'clock," he added.

"At seven you close and lock the gate," said his sister. "And you close it and lock it with what, Nelson?"

"Key."

"So you have a key."

"No."

"Then how did you lock the gate?"

"A woman comes walking," Nelson said. "She lives there." He pointed down the road. "She comes with the key to lock the gate, and then she goes away."

"Five minutes ago."

"Yes."

"So she's five minutes down the road, walking. That's all. Five minutes. So go after her in your jeep and get the key." Again, his sister shook the money and pushed the bills farther through the gate.

"No," said Nelson. "There's nothing I can do." Then he smiled and laughed in a way that might have meant that they were invited to smile and laugh, too.

"Not funny, Nelson," said his sister.

She made suggestions, and he couldn't tell if the way she was speaking to Nelson—as if he were a child, or someone who could be ordered around, badgered, and belittled—was something that had become natural to her after living in South Africa for thirty-three years, or an exception to her ongoing rules of behavior, goaded by exasperation, weariness, and cancer. "Do you have a phone, Nelson?" she asked. "Yes," he said. So why didn't he call the woman with the key? What about calling the park administration, or some kind of dispatcher, who could then call a ranger, who could then show up with the key? Wasn't that obvious? Surely they couldn't be the first park visitors who'd come late to the gate but still needed to get out, who couldn't spend the night camped in their car waiting for morning. This same problem must have happened before. There must be, at Pilanesberg—a major park, heavily visited—provisions for late exits. "Okay," said Nelson. "I can phone."

He went back into the guardhouse. Under the stars, by the gate, his sister sighed bitterly. "Typical," she said. "Everything's mismanaged, a mess, in South Africa. Nobody knows what they're doing."

There was a damp, night smell now, alongside the smell of the veldt he'd gotten familiar with that afternoon. He suggested his sister shut off her headlights and kill her car engine; she said no, that probably wasn't a good idea, because of the lions. He didn't believe lions, or any other predator, would attack them by the gate, but since shutting off the car engine wasn't his decision he didn't argue with her about it. Instead, they passed the time talking about Nelson until he returned and said, "Okay, it's better now."

"What does that mean?" his sister asked. "What did they say? Who did you talk to?"

"Someone is coming with a key."

"When?"

"A person is coming," said Nelson.

"When?"

Nelson shrugged apologetically.

They waited for half an hour. There was nothing to do. He took pictures of Nelson—loud flashes—who posed for him, beyond the mesh of the gate, with martial gravity. His sister asked Nelson how old he was—twenty-eight—where he was from—Venda—if he was married—yes, to a woman in Venda—if he had children—four—if he liked his work—no, but it was better than nothing, which is what he'd done in Venda. "I would like to talk to you about a job," said Nelson, out of the blue. "Is there a job I could have, where you live, something I could do, to make more money?"

"Aha," said his sister. "Can you type at a keyboard?" The answer was no. "Can you read English?" A little. "How far did you go in school?" Just a little. "What skills do you have?" None, said Nelson. "So why don't you go to school to learn computers? That would be a valuable skill to have, Nelson." Because school cost money. "Okay," said his sister, pushing her handful of bills again. "You call a second time and get whoever has a key to come here right now, and then I'll help you with your problem, Nelson. We'll deal with your employment situation."

"There is nothing I can do." Nelson looked exasperated. "I said to you before, you have to wait."

His sister sighed. "Nelson," she said, "this is no way to act. This is unacceptable. You're going to pay for this." She turned a circle in the headlights, turned back to the gate, pressed against it, and again shoved the money through. "Take it," she said. "You have to. I'm telling you to."

"No money."

"What a bad job you have here, Nelson," his sister said. "Don't you want something better paying? Aren't you scared out here, all alone?"

"This is why I have no key," said Nelson. "Trust. There is no trust of me."

"But aren't you scared of robbers? They'll cut your throat, robbers. For two rand."

"No," answered Nelson. "I'm scared of lions. Because when the power is gone, there is no electric fence to stop them from coming right here." He pointed at his feet.

"Great," his sister said. "Where does that leave us?"

Nelson explained that behind them, right behind them, twenty meters wide, was an electric grate. "Don't go there," he added. "It's very bad."

"Now you tell us," his sister said. "Nelson," she added. "You should be fired from your job. I'm going to see to it that you're fired."

But Nelson didn't answer. He rubbed his chin thoughtfully, then his neck, then his forehead. "Okay," he said. "You wait here." He marched into the guardhouse, shut the door, and didn't come back.

They sat in the car for an hour with the sunroof open, the headlights and the motor off, looking at the Southern Hemisphere stars, and he didn't feel impatient. If they weren't here, they'd be somewhere else, so what difference did it make? Here or back at their little chalet, looking at stars from there? "You know what?" he said. "I think we're trapped here. I think we have to make the best of it."

His sister adjusted her seat back farther, the better to take in the stars. This caused her wig to unseat a little, and now, while she spoke, she readjusted it. "Make the best of it," she said, as though it were a novel idea.

"Yes."

"Okay," she said. "We'll make the best of it, then, because what choice do we have? We have none."

At nine, a convoy of open-air minibuses rumbled up behind them, each full of guests who had paid extra for nocturnal sightseeing, through night-vision binoculars, of wildlife. He took pictures of a man wearing complicated goggles with straps and a chin buckle. This was the kind of subject he liked, and he snapped away at it with interest. Then the ranger in the lead minibus leapt out and unlocked the gate, and everybody drove through, including them, while Nelson saluted each driver. When they were abreast of him, his sister opened her window and said, "Sorry, Nelson!" before following the convoy to the Golden Leopard. In their chalet, they freshened up, then went for a celebratory late dinner—celebratory of their liberation from Pilanesberg—on the resort's terrace, which was lit by kerosene torches. But his sister couldn't eat anything and drank water and watched with a hand against her gut while he tucked into a carpaccio of impala served with sliced melon and chilled cottage cheese, followed by an impala T-bone steak, rare, with mushrooms, onions, carrots, and courgettes, and, for dessert, two scones with cream, jam, and a snifter of port. This meal tired him out so completely that in the thatch-roofed hut he could do nothing but sit while his sister lay with a damp towel across her forehead and her wig on a side table.

At dawn, he went out onto the porch with his camera. He liked dawn now, in the middle of his life. There were strange noises in the distance, reverberating thuds that turned out to be baboons knocking over rubbish bins. He watched through his telephoto lens while they drank from a swimming pool. Soon they were nearer, sitting on bins and picking through them with careful fingers, or parked on their asses and licking salt from foil bags. The troop kept coming, the adults deliberate, the young ones gadding in and out, circling. They cruised between the chalets, turning over every bin they found, so close now that he had to retreat inside and watch through a window. One came to the pane and looked at him impassively; he took a dozen pictures of its intricate face as it assessed him with detachment colored by disdain. He wanted to call to his sister to come see, but it was better to let her rest for now, because the good part of her life, at this stage, was rest; everything else left her worn out and agitated. Then the baboons were gone, followed by a pair of meerkats interested in leftovers, and after that by employees of the Golden Leopard, black men in uniforms with name tags on their shirts and plastic bags in hand, who silently—so as not to awaken the tourists in the chalets—righted the bins and picked up the rubbish. He took pictures of them, too, because what else could he do in his situation? What should he do, beyond that?

Politics

The strike began. He went to the lobby with the intention of arranging a taxi to Patan Hospital, but none, said the concierge, were available. Literally, none. So thoroughly unavailable that, if you wanted to leave the country, you had to walk to the airport. And, in fact, a lot of people were doing that, with hired porters carrying their luggage. Nepal was shut down—no banks, shops, cars, trucks, no goods coming in or out of Kathmandu, nothing happening, nothing moving. "How long is this going to last?" he asked the concierge. "I have somewhere I have to go this morning." But the concierge just shrugged and smoothed his eyebrows. "Outside is not good," he warned.

He took matters into his own hands. His ex-wife, a journalist—technically she was still his wife, because they hadn't signed divorce papers yet—had been traveling in the remote east when the car she was a passenger in veered into a bus, killing three people and injuring sixteen, and now she had twenty screws in her pelvis. Her spleen had been removed, but there was concern about tetanus. Erring on the side of caution, he was going to have her transferred to a Level One Trauma Center in Delhi, and that was why he had to get to Patan this morning. Strike or no strike, he was headed there to fill out paperwork and start things moving. In other words, unlike a lot of the Hyatt Regency's guests, he wasn't in Nepal for a trek in the mountains, a rhododendron tour, or a bird-watching expedition—but there was no point in telling the concierge this. So instead he found the "business center"—three battered Dells around a corner from the reception desk—and Google Mapped the shortest walking route to Patan. Seven point eight kilometers—not quite five miles. Two hours at most. With a bottle of water, a hat, and sunscreen, walking would be his answer to this strike. He printed out the map, got his water bottle, hat, and sunscreen from his room, returned to the lobby with these things in hand, and, waving at the concierge, left.

His map, he soon found, was misleading. He wanted, first, to get to the Ring Road—a straight shot, according to Google—but in truth the indicated route, beyond the immediate pale of his hotel, was a maze of muddy alleys full of flies, dog shit, mangy curs, garbage, and—most immediate of all—poor people. The area was called Boudhanath, and according to his guidebook it was full of Buddhist monasteries. Sure enough, he saw monks walking around. The big point of interest in Boudhanath was its gargantuan stupa, which, according to the guidebook, contained relics of the Buddha. That explained the many shops—right now, all with metal roll-doors down—under signs indicating that they sold things for tourists, like Buddha figurines, prayer rugs, prayer flags, incense, postcards, and thangka paintings. At the moment, though, they sold nothing, because of the strike. Instead of selling goods and wares, the merchants were sitting around, and so was everybody else, except for a few kids playing cricket in the street because—for once, he realized—there were no cars and trucks to stop them, except that on occasion someone blasted through on a motorcycle, taking, he supposed, a political chance. Young guys, reckless and cavalier, always with a passenger, sometimes two. As soon as they passed, things fell quiet again. It was a hot morning in early May—dogs asleep in the shade, garbage reeking. And beggars everywhere. Some were lame and sickly, immobile and imploring, but most were urchins who trotted along next to him, trying to look and sound more pathetic than they were. Not that they weren't pathetic. Half naked, unwashed, they naturally and inevitably plucked at his heartstrings. But, still, he wished they wouldn't tap his hip eight thousand times in a row while saying, "Sir, sir, money, money," or otherwise, in their half-intelligible ways, pleading their insistent cases. He decided to pretend that these child-beggars didn't exist, that he didn't hear or see them, but this was even more infuriating, because it embroiled him now in self-examination, and in pondering the conclusion he was rapidly coming to—that you couldn't win in a case like this. That, no matter what you did, you were wrong.

Beset this way, he came to the Ring Road. The Maoists had taken control of it, he could see, by clogging the intersection. In red shirts and bandannas, they milled with restless zeal, listening to a speaker exhort them through a bullhorn. Except for a few motorcycles, some oxcarts, bicyclists, water trucks, and a couple of ambulances, the Ring Road was, for the moment, pedestrians only. In a way, that was lucky: he wouldn't have to dodge traffic. Trying to look full of confidence, bold, he crossed it and pressed on toward the hospital. Now his way felt unimpeded. He'd left the tourist zone of Boudhanath behind, which meant fewer beggars, con men, and touts. Once, he saw an air-conditioned bus coming at him with a large sign on its windshield reading TOURIST ONLY, as if that were a talisman that could thwart tossed rocks. As far as he could tell, the sign was working. The bus seemed to have carte blanche, despite the strike. But then he saw that, behind the bus, there were two jeeps full of soldiers in blue camo fatigues. They had weapons in their hands and slung across their shoulders. On he walked, with sweaty duress, bulling past the frowns of red-shirted teen-agers, some of whom brandished long, thick staves. Troops had taken up positions. Some kept watch behind sandbagged outposts, while others stood or crouched in the shade, or bounced past in fast-moving, canopied carriers. Well, it wasn't his business, whatever was going on. None of this had to do with him. But then he came to what his map called a river—mud, plastic bags, garbage, shit—and the road he was on became a bridge blocked by Maoists. Fortunately, they were letting pedestrians cross, except that, when *he* tried to cross, a caramel-skinned and gaunt, tense teen put a hand on his chest to check his progress. They stood like that, facing each other, the Maoist with his imposing stave, he with his sunscreen, water bottle, and hat. While other pedestrians passed in droves, the reality of his circumstances soon became clear to him: he had to go back, he couldn't cross.

He retreated, but only by fifty yards—back to the first patch of shade he could find—and stood there, wondering if he should get out his wallet, produce a wad of Nepalese rupees, and try, again, to cross the bridge. He was considering this when someone tapped his hip—a boy a little older than the average child-beggar, whose English was coherent but far from perfect. "America," he said. "Have a nice day?"

"No."

"Yes," said the boy. "Not as nice. And now, I clean your shoe."

"No."

"Yes, yes, please," said the boy. "I clean."

He looked at his shoes. Sure enough, as the boy had sought to suggest, there was copious dog shit on one of them. Yellow-brown, shiny, slick, and fresh, and smearing both the sole and the leather below the laces. "Great," he said. "Dog shit."

"I clean," replied the boy. "Please."

They were in front of a shop where, among other things, you could have gotten a vacuum cleaner repaired if there was no strike. It was closed, or nearly closed; the metal roll-door was open about two feet at the bottom to let air in on someone who, he could tell by the clink of tools, was working today. Here the boy pulled two plastic bags from his pocket. With one he made a clean place for his client to sit, spreading and smoothing the plastic fastidiously. Then, just as carefully, he removed the offensive shoe and, holding the shoeless foot up, set the other bag under it, and set the shoeless foot down on that. And so, via two bits of plastic produced from the boy's pocket, his pants seat and sock were buffered from contact with Kathmandu.

He watched. The boy appeared neither humiliated nor disgusted. With the point of a stick, he worked steadily on the dog shit while squatting with an enviable comfort and flexibility that, ubiquitous here, were rare in America. He also had an incredible head of hair, glossy, black, thick, neatly cut. And an unwrinkled, clean, short-sleeved rayon shirt. And clean shoes. And patience. And deft technique with a worn brush and a rag. And he was so thorough about cleaning the shoe that when he was finished there was absolutely no sign of dog shit. Not only that, the shoe looked better than it had for a long time—about the way it had when it came out of the box. Lacing it up, inspecting it, he was impressed by what this boy had accomplished with so little in the way of equipment or tools, impressed enough that he unlaced his other shoe and asked the boy to clean it, too. A deferential waggle of the head; two hands, as if the shoe were made of glass; the boy took the shoe with these signs of subservience and then, silently, moved his plastic protector under the newly shoeless foot. And so the second shoe was cleaned as well, with the same polish, efficiency, attentiveness to detail, and pride as the first. "How much do I owe you?" he asked the boy, who answered, while cleaning his hands by rubbing them together, "Twenty-five rupee."

Twenty-five rupees—a little over thirty cents. "That's a steal," he said, and doled out a hundred. Strangely, the boy looked at it with graphic consternation—the way someone at home might look at a parking ticket. "Please," said the boy. "I am taking one hundred rupee and I am bringing seventy-five rupee. Please," he said again. "You are waiting."

"No, no, no. At home that's called a 'tip.' You get to keep the extra."

The boy didn't argue, but he didn't go away, either. Instead, he began asking personal questions. What city? Bellevue, Washington. Is it near New York? No. What work? LASIK surgery. Lay-sa-lick sur-jur-ee? Helping people see better. How many childrens? Three children, all grown. What are their years? Twenty-six, twenty-four, and twenty-one—no grandchildren. Your wife, you have a peek-chur? No picture of my wife. The boy ran out of queries in this vein and began, instead, to float proper nouns—hopeful points of reference—terse utterances that were meant to provoke, from his American interlocutor, just what response? What was he supposed to say to someone who said to him, simply, "Michael Jackson"? Or "Liberty Statue"? Not knowing what to say, he asked the boy what he did when he wasn't cleaning shoes. Answer: the shoe boy was a student of English, math, and computer programming, but there was no school today, because of the strike. The teachers were either supporters or intimidated. This morning they were either thwarting students who tried to attend or letting them in furtively. A teacher had let the shoe boy through the door, so that he might make solitary use of a computer. But then the teacher had gotten nervous and kicked him out.

"Okay," he said. "So now what?"

"Now," said the boy, "I help you walk."

"What?"

"We go," said the boy. "This way."

They used alleys that weren't shown on his map and, around two bends, crossed the "river" on a footbridge of well-traveled pallets planted in a wallow. Then, having detoured, they returned to the main road, well out of sight of the Maoist blockade. "Good one," he told the boy. "Great."

He thought about doling out another hundred rupees. Two hundred rupees? He was in the midst of such deliberations when the boy touched his arm and called his attention to a man with a rag around his head. "Shoe man," the boy said. "He have? He have the shoe box."

"Shoe box?"

"Everything shoe box."

He looked. The man with the rag around his head had in front of him a rather elaborate-looking shoe-cleaning kit full of brushes, sticks, wires, polishes, rubs, rags, waxes, and oils. It was built like a large suitcase, foldable, with a strap. A clever contraption that made his business portable. He could easily purvey services and take it home with him each night.

"Looks convenient," he said to the boy. "But you're better than he is without any 'shoe box.' You're a shoe-shining fool, man, when it comes right down to it." This seemed the right time to reach for his wallet, and as he did so he added, feeling a little jaunty, "It's early and you don't have school today. What will you do with your temporary freedom? Shine shoes? Homework? What's up?"

The boy replied that he was going home to his mother, two sisters, and two younger brothers, but not to his father, because his father was in their village in India while the boy and his mother and siblings were in Kathmandu. His father, he explained, couldn't come with them, because he had a job making bricks in Bihar. Then the boy pointed down a hill to their left. In a field of rubble and garbage, beyond which stood buildings that looked bombed out, was a camp where people lived under tarps, plastic, and cardboard. "I am there," he said. "My family."

So this was the boy's turnoff. That's what he was saying. He was saying that it was time for them to part. And this was fine, since, in his opinion, now was the time to do so. "Goodbye," he said, but the boy replied, "You are meet my family, please. Sit down, drink a tea. Please, you come."

"No."

"Tea," said the boy.

"I don't want tea."

"Please," said the boy. "You greet my mother."

"Sorry. No."

"Please," said the boy. "You buy me the shoe box."

"How much is a shoe box?"

"Please, you have give me seven thousand rupee. For—"

"Jesus," he said, because, in the end, this was about something like eighty-five dollars and not about anything else. Which was too bad, because, until now, the episode had been affecting. He'd even imagined, in its midst, how he might speak of it in glowing terms when he returned home, how he would describe it as a positive experience to his kids and associates, how he would refer to it with his nurse and receptionist. But not now, because what had seemed so positive had swiftly collapsed. It had gotten entangling, irritating, difficult. "Look," he said. "I've enjoyed our meeting. You did a great job with the shoes and the route finding. But, sorry, I have to move on now. So okay. So long. Thanks."

Yet the boy stayed at his side as he walked—at a faster, all-business, I'm-done-with-you pace—saying, repeatedly, "You buy me shoe box."

"Go home," he shouted finally. "I mean it, now. Shoo!" He waved a hand menacingly. "Go on, get out of here. Vamoose!"

For a half-second he gleaned, in the boy's face, disappointment. But then, this kid was going to get over it quickly. He was obviously indefatigable, irrepressible, and intrepid; he was young, optimistic, and a budding entrepreneur who'd recover his confidence and equilibrium. A wonderfully handsome kid, in his way, with skin as perfect as his hair; he had the whole package, he was going places, at least by Nepal's standards. But right now, transparently, he was covering a wound, trying to conceal it from an American who could, for his part, tell what the kid was thinking. He was thinking he didn't deserve this dismissal. He was thinking this American was angry with him. But the American in question wasn't angry at all; it was more that he no longer had patience for the shoe-box insistence. He had things to do; he had to get moving. "Sorry," he said. "I'm not buying you a shoe box." Then he dug out his wallet and showed the boy a thousand rupees. "But here's a start," he added.

Without waiting for a response, he put the money in the boy's hand, then wheeled away quickly and, without looking back, went on toward the hospital.

His ex-wife was watching the strike on television—on the television he'd rented for her, the day he'd arrived, without asking her or saying a word about it: a television as his unspoken gift—and sweating beneath a large ceiling fan. She looked better than she had the afternoon before—less peaked, yellow, black-and-blue, but not less glazed by pain meds. Despite everything—the green hospital gown, the swollen cheeks, the greasy hair, and the gauze taped over one ear—she still looked good to him, and he was still attracted to her style and manner: to her attitude, he supposed was how to put it, or to her ambience, maybe. To the feeling she communicated. To whatever it was that had brought him to her in the first place, when they were both just twenty-three. Here she was in her ravaged condition, trashed and battered, bruised, stitched, and trussed, and he still felt the same tone and tenor of attraction. Soon after they'd met, they'd become caretakers on a tree farm; mornings, there was frost on the inside of their cabin windows, and as a result, they'd alternated—one morning, he would get the fire going in the woodstove before jumping back in bed to wait with her for the temperature to rise, and the next morning, it was her turn to light the fire. It hadn't mattered, to him, whose morning it was, and he still felt the same at Patan Hospital.

His ex-wife had been thrown from a car—had passed through its windshield as the engine was crushed—but fortunately she'd been hurtling upward when she'd hit the bus; otherwise, she'd told him, she'd be dead. Not that she remembered her fortuitous angle—it was, rather, that a doctor had explained all this to her, as a conjecture based on the nature of her injuries. The same doctor who'd put twenty screws through her pelvis after she'd been airlifted to Patan from the east, where she'd gone to cover the Maoist insurgency out of journalistic curiosity. Did people in the east support the Maoists, or were they just intimidated enough to go along with the comprehensive strikes, called by Maoists, that so regularly brought this country to a halt? How did they feel there? What was their take on things? A strike had been called for—the one that was on now—and she'd been trying to get ahead of it with reporting from remote locations. Then—bam.

What did the Maoists want? he asked her. Why were they striking? And, while they were on this subject, wasn't the term "Maoist" anachronistic? His ex-wife said that the Maoists would operate under a different name if the response of the West was important to them, but the response of the West was not important. What their leaders wanted was for the prime minister to step down, because he'd failed to call a vote on a constitution. They wanted Maoists equitably distributed among the ranks of the military, where right now they had "tons of foot soldiers," as she put it, "but zero officers." One more thing: they wanted not to share power, as they sometimes claimed, but to have it all, to get rich and live high while stepping on the throats of other people. This last point, she emphasized, was her take on things, arrived at from her perspective as a journalist who'd covered the Maoists for seven months. In other words, since they'd separated.

Then it was time for him to broach the subject he'd come there to broach. What about transferring to Delhi for proper treatment? "Proper treatment meaning what?" she asked.

"Treatment on a par with treatment in the West. The treatment you'd get at home—good treatment."

"No," she answered. "I don't want that."

She was compromised by meds, he told himself again, irrational because of pain pills and a sedative. And, given this fact, it was his job to think straight, act on her behalf, advocate for her, and make the right things happen. "You need to go to Delhi," he insisted. "And then you need to come home for a while. Rest, rehab, physical therapy. Take stock, retrench, reload, all of that. That's just how things turned out."

"No, they didn't."

"Yes, they did."

"I'm not insured to go to Delhi," she said. "I can't afford to go to Delhi."

He shrugged at this, looking at her skeptically. "You know as well as I do—right?—that I've totally and completely got you covered," he said. "Money shouldn't be a deal breaker."

"I don't want your money," she replied.

He went on trying, but she wouldn't take his largesse. No matter what he tried, no matter how he argued it. She wasn't going to convalesce in Delhi, or rehab at home, where he lived, in Bellevue. Finally, a nurse came and gave her another sedative, and gradually his ex-wife receded from conversation. For a while he watched the strike on television. The Maoists were demonstrating in Durbar Square and outside the Narayanhiti Royal Palace. They were burning tires and setting up barricades. Banging their staves against the palace gates. Chanting and throwing rocks at the police. He mulled these images of chaos for a while, and when he turned to look at his ex-wife again, her eyes were closed and her tongue was lolling. Maybe it was time for him to leave.

It was a long return walk to the Hyatt Regency, but he

made it without confrontation or difficulty. The trouble had moved to the north and west, leaving him a clear path to Boudhanath, which was good, because he really couldn't deal with one more exasperating, frustrating hassle of the sort that was inevitable in Nepal. He made it to his room and turned on the air conditioning. Then he showered, ordered a hamburger and fries, and dined in privacy, where no one could bother him. The fries, he thought, were seasoned with something interesting. That, he supposed, was the Third World trade-off. You put up with shit for a taste of the exotic. But the truth was that the fries didn't taste good, because nothing did when you ate by yourself. Solitude having undercut his appetite, he opened his door and set his tray down in the hallway. His pile of fries and half a burger were discovered by a bellboy, who ate them in a service elevator, pondering, not for the first time since he'd gained this coup of a job, why guests didn't finish meals. What sort of people were these hotel guests? the bellboy wondered. What was in their hearts and minds? He was fascinated by Westerners, especially Western women, who made him feel self-conscious and embarrassed. In his fantasy life he made love to them, and they showered him with—what else?—money. At ten thousand rupees per kiss.

Feedback

Her older daughter was doing clinical training in music therapy at the University of Minnesota, and her younger daughter worked in a Bolivian medical clinic. Her husband was at a three-day symposium on team building in Los Altos. In other words, she had time, which was good, since she was behind on letters of recommendation, on personal reading, on professional reading, on two sets of American civil rights movement quizzes that needed grades and a set of Jim Crow era essays that needed comments, on the adult-literacy curriculum she was putting together for a nonprofit, on thank-you notes, and on research for a book she'd long wanted to write on wage discrimination against women. And—as always—behind on exercise. What came first? She had perfectly good reasons to procrastinate on the exercise, to stay home, feet up, with her couch as her workstation, and phone, text, e-mail, draft, scribble, record, and put entries in her plan book, all the while a little gloomily aware that she hadn't walked since Wednesday, that it was now Sunday, that today it was essential, even mandatory, to walk—this sort of troubled thinking about exercise lay under her other thoughts until, late in the afternoon, at the last practical hour really—in January it was dark by five—she finally got up from the couch.

She went out wearing the hat she'd just finished knitting and the new winter boots she felt dubious about. Were they going to break in or should she return them? They were warm enough but their toe boxes felt tight. In these uncomfortable boots, then, she walked to the park, where the trees were all leafless and, because of the cold, no people were present. What was the temperature? Fifteen? Twenty? She took the gravel path toward the frozen pond, crossed, gingerly, the icy footbridge, and power-walked beside the synthetic-turf soccer field, where no nets were up, and where the lines regulating the game were blurred and frosted over. All still, all silent, but then, as she passed the concession stand—closed for the winter—a car turned into the rec-area parking lot. Whoever it was, he or she didn't get out right away. The motor went on running—rising, white exhaust. Finally a guy emerged and, standing beside his door, waved in the manner of someone who knew her, of someone friendly and familiar. Who was it, waving like that—waving with so much odd enthusiasm? She couldn't tell from her distance. She could see that he wore a lime-green parka and—she thought—a stocking cap. He was well bundled up, that much was obvious. She was terrible with cars; all she could say about his was that it was small, one of those blunt and truncated-looking gas savers, beside which the guy looked, maybe, taller than he was as he hailed her with such strange animation, his right hand waggling at the end of his wrist and raised to about eye level. Was this somebody she knew? An acquaintance of some kind? She pulled one hand from her pocket and, as he'd done, raised it to eye level, like someone taking an oath, or like a student uncertain of the answer she's about to make, and waved back in her way, no waggling, measured, all her probity intact—not that she had more probity than the next person—and her enthusiasm checked, just in case. Because, after all, she didn't want to issue an invitation—come here, stand beside me, let's chat, we're friends—that wasn't her intention. But what was her intention? Her intention was unclear, she didn't know what she meant to say with her stiff and reserved wave—I'm receptive but I'm not receptive, thank you but no thank you. Certainly, she felt, she should at the very least do nothing offensive; to leave him unacknowledged was maybe a mistake, or even a danger. What's wrong? he might think, don't you say hi to people? On the other hand, maybe it would have been safer to pretend she hadn't seen him, whoever he was, stranger or friend, familiar or unfamiliar, threatening opportunist or amiable acquaintance. Who was it, greeting her so aggressively? Maybe only someone on an even keel today and in a good winter mood, someone not subject to seasonal affective disorder, someone with a generous and outgoing outlook or equipped with outsized social graces, maybe this was just park etiquette, lonely park etiquette, It's me, a stranger, but no one to worry about, Happy New Year, have a nice day. Enough worry! she thought, as he reached into his car for something. She saw only his upper back as he dug around for it. The exhaust stopped rising; he'd killed his motor. Then he emerged with a phone in hand, which he held to his ear while opening a rear door. A lapdog on a leash jumped out, and the two of them began walking toward her with the guy pressing his phone to his ear and the dog taking fast, tiny steps.

What was this about? What did it mean, the wave, then a call? You're important, I'm glad to see you; you've dazzled me, you're nothing, you're wonderful . . . but . . . wait . . . okay . . . I have thirty seconds between greeting you with a wave and saying hi at close quarters, why not use it productively, check off a phone call, the message I'm sending you is—but, what was his message? It was definitely bizarre, his inordinate good cheer, his theatrical animation, his mincing dog, this guy now closing distance with his phone in one hand and his leash in the other, talking away even while the dog gave a tug and stopped so it could squat over the stiff grass, the guy turning to look in the direction of the pond and then in the opposite direction, surveying the park and, she thought, wondering if anyone besides her had noticed that he wasn't getting down on his knees with a plastic mitt or a pooper scooper, after that evaluating the clouds as if his guilt-laden reconnaissance were part of a general love of nature—doing that for her sake—or maybe he was doing what people do in winter as the day gets on, because they're worried—she was worried—about worsening weather and early darkness, not wanting to get caught out past a certain point, say four-thirty, that was about the right time to start home in January if you were out for a walk, maybe she could check her phone to see what time it was—but wouldn't that be rude, to pull out her phone? No. People were always pulling out their phones, it didn't have to mean anything. And he was on his phone. And yes, he was wearing a stocking cap, which was weird, too, although didn't he have a right, in this weather, to a stocking cap? Or maybe, she thought, it was actually called a watch cap, the kind sailors wore on watch in cold weather, that was probably why it was called a watch cap though it was also the cap that thieves wore in movies, or rather burglars, cat burglars—black stretch pants, black turtleneck, black watch cap—while slipping noiselessly through a bedroom window one leg after the other. Was there a creepier hat than the hat this guy wore? The one with the eyeholes was definitely creepier; she couldn't remember what it was called right now, how tempting it was to pull out her phone and—anyway, he wasn't wearing that. He was wearing a watch or stocking cap, black, he put away his phone, his dog finished up, the two of them once more advanced. A guy in a lime-green parka, leading his little dog toward her and raising his hand again in that more than just slightly enthusiastic wave.

She could see who he was now. It was Hamish McAdam, Hamish McAdam whose name used to make her privately laugh because "hamish," to her, a Jewish girl, sort of—in adulthood she'd divested herself of Jewishness—meant, in Yiddish—spelled "haimish"—warm and cozy. How could there be a Hamish McAdam? A Yiddish-invoking first name and a Scottish last name, those didn't go together and made you think, merged—or made her think, anyway—of a clansman in a kilt and a yarmulke. She thought of Hamish McAdam every semester when she put the word "macadam" up on Power-Point among other Industrial Revolution terms—spinning jenny, flying shuttle, steam engine, seed drill, macadam, a new type of road construction. Hamish McAdam? Hamish McAdam had taught photography and science, and had once been celebrated because, as a hobby, and involving kids, he'd installed a weather station on the school's roof that not only collected data but got mentioned, many evenings, on a television news show by a meteorologist rolling through suburbs and towns, rain, wind, and temperatures. People'd thought well of Hamish because of that, Hamish who'd built this weather station on his own dime, Hamish who gave extra time to his students, Hamish who, in the faculty room, happily ate his lunch among women while the other guy teachers held down guy tables. Hamish who kept a fishbowl in his classroom, balanced his checkbook with an overkill graphing calculator, ate a warm cafeteria cookie with a carton of milk or worked a crossword puzzle during morning break. Hamish who wore, in his hair, or what was left of it, shiny gel, so that it stood up like gleaming bristles. Hamish who fought the weight battle openly, noting aloud the fat and carb content of items and assisting others with conspicuously fast conversions of nutritional-content information—grams to ounces, milligrams, milliliters. His signature wardrobe—argyle sweater vest, cuffed cords, plaid socks, and saddle shoes—had always seemed, to her, too studied, but really, if she was fair, who wasn't studied when it came to self-furnishings? Hamish was crisp, well cropped, gelled, clean-shaven, cheery, and a pleasant enough faculty presence, until, one day—maybe five years ago, she thought—he'd left the building "on probation" while an investigation into allegations of wrongdoing went forward,

the wrongdoing along the lines of inappropriate involvement
with a student, which no one knew anything about but which
everyone, meaning all the teachers in their building, discussed
anyway, vigorously and speculatively, based on what little the
principal had revealed to this or that faculty or staff member; those small bits of "fact" made the rounds and gathered
together until a full-blown rumor factory was up and running,
all of this before blogs and social media had become so power-
ful that surmises and allegations could go viral and that way
become, at high speed, vehement and ridiculous. Rumors about
Hamish became vehement and ridiculous with less digital
help; it had been mostly old-school at school; exponential word
of mouth. Was it 2005? She thought it might have been 2005,
the Hamish-McAdam-might-be-a-perv-gossip-fest, because,
she remembered, that was the year the district went on strike
and there were plenty of meetings and a lot of downtime and
talk, some of that talk about the issues behind striking—pay,
mainly, higher pay—and some of it about Hamish McAdam.
Hamish McAdam, one of their union reps but not present at meetings, not present, apparently, because something
had happened, but what was that something, the details? It
was said, it was thought—the story went, anyway—that the
weather station on the roof called for regular monitoring, that
Hamish had established a rotation of students to go up there,
carefully, with a key and safety measures, for the purpose of
checking and maintaining equipment, of taking notes—of
learning things—that these were his hand-picked, favorite
students, girls and boys but mostly girls, because Hamish's
favorite students were girls—he had a girl, each semester, as

a "teacher's aide," always a girl, to enter grades in his book and do other small but necessary things—and that some of these stints involved evening visits for purposes related to relative humidity or some such twilit or dark-of-night phenomenon, no one really knew, but anyway, summer evenings on the roof, beneath the moon, under stars, with Hamish sometimes unexpectedly on hand offering snacks, soft drinks, and a telescope on a tripod, which he invited his student monitors to look through and . . . and . . . it was in this meteorological and star-gazing context that something had either happened or not happened, no one knew, because the district office, the principal, the vice-principals, anyone with information was only willing to say, officially, that the matter was under investigation, while adding, privately, a tidbit here and there—those informal asides and "you didn't hear it from me"s that formed the basis of rampant speculation during, indeed it was, the strike of 2005.

Soon Hamish was no longer in the building. She hadn't seen him since. But now here he was, in his parka, with his dog, crossing the frozen grass in her direction, smiling, calling out her name, and interrupting, in his jovial way, her exercise regimen. Or, rather, not interrupting it, because she refused to stop, why should she stop, she didn't want to exchange pleasantries or feign ignorance of his troubles, there were so few opportunities for getting her heart rate up and keeping it there. "Unbelievable!" said Hamish, when their paths converged. "It's freezing!"

She saw that he'd aged in a way common to Scotsmen—namely, he'd not only grown dangerously stouter but had distinctly more broken capillaries in his cheeks so that his face had a blue and dappled tint. His puffy parka, nearly fluorescent, made him look ample and segmented. His dog leash, maroon, had a woven print—stars—and his dog, though tiny, pulled against it, toward her legs, while Hamish, at the other end, resisted. "Pepper!" he snapped, looking delighted and proprietary. "Pepper! No! It's a friend!" Then he bent, not without difficulty, scooped up Pepper, and pinned him or her beneath his billowy arm. "I'm sorry," he said, with a gasp.

"It's fine," she said, still walking.

In the long-winded, unable-to-cut-to-the-chase way she recalled from their era as colleagues, Hamish explained that at Christmas he'd gone for two weeks to Kauai with his mother, two sisters, and six nieces and nephews, leaving Pepper in a dog-boarding facility he couldn't recommend because Pepper, on his return, seemed unduly anxious, so that now some pieces of her careful training were undone, he was engaged in certain repetitions with Pepper of behavioral steps she'd succeeded with already, meanwhile he apologized again for this episode of lunging, and with that, Hamish put Pepper on the turf once more—delicately—stroked her neck, sighed, and said, pre-emptively, "Pepper, Pepper, Pehhhhhh-prrrrrr?"

By what unhappy coincidence had she ended up here with dog and man? A circumstance Hamish could have handled—and that she wished he would have handled—by ignoring her, by pretending not to recognize her, which is how most people would have handled it, out of a basic feel for the propriety called for given the elements at hand—late Sunday afternoon, super-cold, a walk, they hardly knew each other.

What should she say? She wanted him to leave. She wished he hadn't shown up in the first place, or that, having shown up, he'd been sensitive enough to social norms not to accost her in this sustained way—Just get on with walking your Pepper, she thought, hurry up, Hamish, we'll greet in passing and go opposite directions, you toward the play area, the footbridge, and the pond, me toward the Park Department mulch and compost heaps and the community-garden patches. "How have you been?" Hamish asked.

Enough! she decided—more than enough! And didn't she have an excuse to be brusque? Maybe more than one excuse? "The thing is," she said, "as slow as I look, and I'm really sorry, but this is an exercise walk for me and I have to keep moving because I time myself, okay? I'm really, really sorry, Hamish."

He stopped; she stopped; Pepper, as ineffectually as before, attacked her legs, and Hamish, dragging the dog out of her range by its leash, said, with a knit unibrow, "I get it. Okay. Another time."

"Great," she said. "Nice seeing you." And went her way.

What do you do after such an encounter? After walking another 1.6 miles with a falling feeling of social remorse? And having lied about timing yourself? You go home and Google "Hamish McAdam." Which is what she did, and got, in order, a Hamish McAdam who lived in New Zealand, Hamish McAdamses with Facebook pages, a Hamish McAdam in Canada, a young Hamish McAdam who played lacrosse, and eventually, on page two, there was the Hamish McAdam she knew but wished she didn't. He had a photography Web site, which she didn't go to just yet, opting instead for a look at him in Google Images—in the third row, a picture of a flabby, sunburned Hamish sitting on the edge of a deck lounger beside a pool with a drink and a newspaper on the little table beside him, and behind him were those jacarandas? She realized, A, that it didn't matter if they were jacarandas, and B, that she felt really bad for having blown him off. She'd been mean, which was ironic, because she wasn't mean, she moved through the world trying not to be mean, mainly because it was better in the moral sense, but also because it was easier. Making a big deal about things, taking a stand, getting emotional, getting assertive, insisting, reacting, making someone else's problem your problem—she felt she was good at avoiding all of that, but this time, with Hamish, she'd slipped and, without meaning to, basically just blown it when it came to a social encounter. What to do? There was nothing to do except to relearn a lesson she wished she didn't have to relearn but had already relearned a number of times: never do anything that might make you feel bad. That was all. So simple and obvious. She let it sink in. She was hungry now—walking made her hungry—but still felt bad about Hamish McAdam, bad enough that leaving her laptop didn't make sense yet, she could still take a look at his Web site, at the photography he did, maybe that would yield something, hopefully some sort of confirmation that in fact she was not a bad human being—except maybe first she should start a carbonara and boil water for some farfalle, interweaving that with looking at the photographs Hamish took. Except that she'd made a deal with herself not to multitask, a deal she found herself breaking not only often but even daily, even hourly, even minute by minute. It was only when she realized it—that she was multitasking again—that she found herself able, briefly, to do one thing at a time, but then it was back to fiddling with her Web page on one side of the screen while building a spreadsheet on the other, or talking on the phone while Googling, which reminded her of something: that she should call or e-mail, who would be best, Les Gross, Dane Snow, John Herringer, all three? Guess what? I ran into Hamish McAdam in the park, he's gained fifteen pounds and has a lapdog! No. She wouldn't write that. Anyway, here was his Web site, a little on the cheap side—not tacky, just thread-bare, not embarrassing, just bare-bones—bare-bones such that, in a stretch, you could decide that it was the product of an intentional minimalism instead of—this was probably what it really was—lack of funds. No audio, no video, links to four galleries, Home, News, About, Contact, and the photos themselves, divided into portfolios—The Natural World, Portraits, Projects, Fine Art, Candid Lifestyle. She looked under Candid Lifestyle. Kids leaping through a sprinkler.

News? That seemed laughable. How could there be news about Hamish McAdam, other than old news—that he'd lost his teaching job because of whatever it was with a student? She clicked on News. Bare but for the italicized announcement that Hamish's show, "Feedback," was "on view" at the Nash Gallery. She knew the Nash Gallery. A hole in the wall. Time to start the carbonara, but not before forwarding this page to Les Gross, Dane Snow, Gail North, and John Herringer—almost the entire Social Studies Department—along with the message *Ran into Hamish M. Check it out. Feedback?*

In the morning she woke with less guilt in her system. Only after she had been awake for ten minutes did she even remember that she'd blown off Hamish. Night had laid the matter under a little. Night had intervened. Good, she thought. Let more time pass. Was it really that big of a deal?

Downstairs, she noticed something that had escaped her all weekend. Her husband, who had been raised in a mildly Presbyterian family of, actually, atheists and agnostics—except for a sister who'd married an Egyptian and, via that, become Baha'i—had left a messy heap of bicycle-riding things by the garage door. There were his lobster gloves, Windstopper, winter biking shoes, and thermal bib tights. The gear, on the floor, left like that while he was gone in Los Altos, irritated her, but also made her miss his coffee. He did a very patient pour-over. He was also good at scones, adding small touches such as lemon rind or gingered plum. Gear on the floor was irresponsible, but she decided not to talk to him about it. She ate toast, drank French press, checked e-mail, checked news, checked messages, and pondered her Web page, the assignments there, the questions to be answered, the readings, the dates for quizzes and tests, the dates papers were due, she was in the middle of that when a schedule reminder popped up—a reminder that today was, for her, an observation day, meaning that an administrator was going to sit in on one of her classes for the purpose of what she knew to be a perfunctory evaluation of her merits as a teacher, perfunctory because she'd been a teacher for twenty-three years and had a track record, so that today's visit was really just a matter of one of two vice-principals, or maybe the principal, Mark Mitchell—"Marky Mark," as her students had branded him, though some called him Eminem instead—sitting at the back of her room for fifty minutes, afterward writing up something complimentary and approving and putting it in her file, but not before giving her a copy at a meeting that would last no more than ten minutes and cover other things, who knew what, there was always one crisis or another in the building and often more than one. Right now it was pain over budget cuts, because no one wanted to be told they were deserving of the ax first, if, as was presently the case, the ax had to fall. She and whichever administrator would talk about hurt feelings in the building, not about her teaching. If it was Mark, the meeting would be uncomfortable because she'd openly disdained him almost from day one; if it was . . . But then her mind went back to the fact that she'd blown off Hamish in the park.

It was indeed Mark. She always thought of him as clueless—he gave off an aura of conspicuous cluelessness—even while he said all of the right things about everybody and about the social-studies curriculum. He summarized for her, sometimes, books he was reading—most recently one on social media and bullying. Before that on adolescent girls as intellectually undervalued; before that on how American society had, as he put it, "turned" on its children. Did he believe America had turned on its children? Probably not. Probably he thought *she* believed it. Now here he was in the back of her room, wearing a V-necked sweater with a hefty twill, greeting students by nodding at them—raised chin—and sitting, she felt, with over-the-top rectitude.

She performed—not that it mattered. She asked: Is affirmative action good or bad? What is the ethical basis for it? What—exactly—did federal law say about it? How did it relate to the Civil Rights Act of 1964? Is affirmative action constitutionally legitimate? When discussion flagged, she read, aloud, the Equal Protection Clause of the Fourteenth Amendment. Then she asked whether affirmative action should be a federal or a state matter. What did students think about state initiatives prohibiting affirmative-action programs? Constitutional or not? If so, on what basis? What about quotas—what did they think of quotas? Specifically quotas for entrance to universities? A student wanted to know what the difference was between a university and a college. She let Mark answer that, because he wanted to—she let him be a font of that sort of knowledge. Then she steered things back. Weigh two goods, she said, not a good and a bad. One good was greater diversity in classrooms, the other an equal playing field. One good was repair of the damages of history, the other a rigorous fairness in the moment. She assigned Title VI of the Civil Rights Act—read by tomorrow—and a brief essay, due Friday: *Should institutions of higher learning be allowed to use race as a factor in determining admissions? Why or why not?* The bell rang.

At the beginning of lunch, she checked messages and e-mail. Gail had replied to all about Hamish: *Thanks for sending, viewed with interest.* So had Les Gross: *Très avant-garde.* And so had John Herringer: *Hamish!*

She forgot about Hamish. Or thought about him with a less intense regret. Her husband came home. No exercise, he said, while in Los Altos, except for twenty minutes in a hotel gym. He went for a bike ride, she for a walk. Walking engaged something neuronal, she thought, because while she was doing it her regret increased again. But only temporarily. She and her husband did their weekly face-time with their daughter in Bolivia, he stiffly, she with bemusement. They both felt she didn't know what she was doing. They talked about her while putting dinner together. The two girls were different, though both were filled with social purpose. The older more deliberate, the younger more rash. The older calmer, the younger more passionate. And the older more likely to get married and have children. The younger might end up so dedicated to her work that she would never return from . . . was it "the developing world"? Her husband had no problem with the phrase, but herself, she'd never liked it.

She checked e-mail. DMW. For years they'd passed this code back and forth—she, Les Gross, Dane Snow, John Herringer, Gail North—and now Sarah Holger, new to the department: DMW, Department Meeting Wednesday, meaning drinks after work on short notice. Usually just a glass of wine somewhere, often in the living room of someone's home, but sometimes in a restaurant or a wine bar. Every December, on the Wednesday before Winter Break, the Social Studies Department tippled together festively, and every June, on the last Wednesday of the school year, it celebrated with wine. Then there were the DMWs when, without an excuse, some of them drank too much, including her, because she didn't want to seem superior to her colleagues. For that reason, she sometimes drank three or four Wednesday glasses of wine, even though they gave her a headache.

Les Gross drove. They convened—a first—at Sarah Holger's loft. She found out, there, that Sarah was twenty-seven. They met Sarah's dog. They were offered a choice of playlists, which led to a discussion of iTunes Radio, and then a demonstration of iTunes Radio, everyone choosing, together—by consensus—urban humming stereo. Sarah served kale chips in an acacia-wood bowl and, because people were curious, Jell-O shots. They were undrinkable—again by consensus—but Sarah had wine on hand as well. Something in all of this made her decide to go for it. There were amalgamating factors: Sarah had a magnum left over from the holiday season that, once opened, needed to be emptied; Les Gross was driving; she'd taken a longer walk than usual the day before; for the moment—however ephemeral—she was less behind than she usually felt; and finally, she hadn't yet shown the new kid—Sarah—this side of herself. "Sure," she said, whenever Sarah poised the magnum. "Why not?"

Near-universal kudos for Sarah's part of town—gentrified without losing all of its rough edges, fun without feeling like a theme park for whites—followed by Sarah's mirthful scoffing about it: after all, every three minutes a lanky, lone white guy could be relied on to walk into Bakery X for a pastry and some face time with a hand-held device after having navigated, as if preoccupied, around an idealist with a clipboard. "It's all good," said Sarah—generalized mockery. She was dating a Sri Lankan woman who worked in the mayor's office. There was some actual business—curriculum-review scheduling—that was quickly dispatched before Department Meeting Wednesday ended with a flurry of sarcastic Mark Mitchell comments. That was their way. They meant nothing by it. Most of the time they were relatively serious. None of them, she believed, only went through the motions. Les, maybe, to some extent—Les struggled openly with burnout.

They were in the car again, she and Les, a block away, before, in her fog, she realized that, somehow, they'd forgotten about Hamish. "Hey!" she said. "We didn't rag on Hamish!"

"We should make up for that," Les advised. "Let's check out whatchamacallit. 'Feedback.' "

"God!" she answered. "Great idea!"

Their mirth endured. They only got control of it outside the Nash's door. A hole in the wall, yes, but inside, it meandered. Around a first corner, still swimming, she felt quieted. They stood before a wall plaque, reading about Hamish:

HAMISH MCADAM

Hamish McAdam was born in Dillingham, Alaska. His father was a bush pilot, his mother a state legislator. McAdam exhibited an early mathematical precocity and an interest in daguerreotype photographic process. As a student at the Brooks Institute in Santa Barbara, he wrote extensively on the daguerreotype revival. In 1984, McAdam introduced his daguerreotype portraiture in Carmel, launching his career as a photographic artist. His work has since appeared in numerous publications, including *Dwell, Flaunt,* and *Photograph* magazine. Currently, McAdam teaches photography at Grosvenor College.

They rounded a second corner. Now the photographs came into view, hung against desiccated if well-cleaned brick. Les went immediately to scrutinize one, while she stayed behind, reading about "Feedback":

FEEDBACK

"Feedback" is a study in infinite regress as it relates to self-reference. Consider, for example, a Morton Salt box, with its image of a girl beneath an umbrella, walking in the rain and carrying, in the crook of one arm, a Morton Salt box. The image both perturbs and intrigues us with its suggestion of a receding infinity.

In audio feedback—a microphone too close to a loudspeaker—an ear-piercing screech comes seemingly out of nowhere. A vicious circle has been set up. Sound entering the microphone is enlarged by the loudspeaker; this larger sound is picked up by the microphone, which transmits it to the loudspeaker, which . . .

Video feedback conforms to the same principle. A camera, connected to a monitor, is rigorously pointed at it, so that the two "experience" each other. Here again we find an infinite regress and an apparently endless self-reference. In "Feedback," this phenomenon is subjected to extended exploration via focal point, contrast, and human intervention—specifically, the interposing of human facial expression. It is a way of looking, ultimately, at "self."

—Hamish McAdam

She looked for forty-five minutes. In each photograph, Hamish had turned his camera on a monitor, and then, between them, interposed a human subject. Faces, eternally multiplied, became helical, or spiraled, or a hub for spokes that were also faces, or like the petals of a flower, but these visual complications only served to clarify expression—perturbation, depression, distress, rage, admonition, mockery. Hamish, whose daguerreotype days appeared to be over, shot in bald and garish light. His people were flagrant. You could see all their blemishes. He exposed them as assailed, as vulnerable.

She had the postmortem with Mark in the midst of her hangover. It was Thursday, a little warmer, and raining heavily. There would be no walking this afternoon. Behind Mark, on his credenza, a photograph of him and his wife looking like the Republicans they were on vacation in Mexico; another of the Mitchell family taken in a studio against a dark-blue backdrop. Mark handed her a copy of his evaluation, which she folded, unread, and slid into her bag. His actual subject: Clement Grimaldi's tearful objections to the excising of Drawing III from the curriculum. Not a judgment, he added. Instead, by the numbers. No class in the building had lower enrollments. Clement could be emotional, he was emotional, he was recently divorced, he'd been ill with a MRSA infection, he took things personally, Clement was an artist. Mark clicked his pen a few times as he spoke. "What do you think?" he asked her. "You've been in this building for a long time."

She knew what to say. She said, "I'm not sure what being an artist has to do with it. Clement is a friend of mine. I like and respect him, but he has a hard time with reality. I agree—he takes things personally."

She thought of something. "Speaking of artists," she said, "Les and I went to the Nash yesterday to see Hamish McAdam's photographs. Remember Hamish? He's teaching somewhere"—she had forgotten where—"I would guess low-residency."

"Not low-residency. He's at Grosvenor College."

"I wonder how he got in front of students again."

"Well, we certainly did what we could to help him. Oh," said Mark, "that stuff. Yeah. It went nowhere, contrary to . . . hearsay."

She didn't answer. Mark took it as an invitation. "We even tried to bring him back," he said. "Wouldn't do it. Fortunately, he didn't bring suit against the district. Not that he would have won, necessarily, but it could have been a much bigger hassle."

"How so?" she asked.

"False allegations. Admitted to. In writing. By a girl I'm not going to name—she made an error. I thought faculty knew all about this," said Mark. "I assumed you knew. Nothing," he stressed. "Hamish never did a single thing wrong. Other than being a little . . . different."

That night she told her husband about Hamish. They were in bed with books; he was about to pull the beaded chain on his lamp. He listened to her story without interruption, and then said that maybe she was obsessing about nothing and that probably, in the end, there'd been little or no harm. Why do you do this to yourself? he asked. Is it going to make the situation better? A situation—his real point—that wasn't even a situation? The guy in the park had probably forgotten it—probably forgot it within a few minutes. It didn't even exist, her husband suggested, except as thoughts in her head.

Feedback

On Friday, she handed back the American civil rights movement quizzes and the set of Jim Crow era essays. The last bell of the week finally rang. She sat down and looked at the weekend weather, the starting times of movies, the hours the pool was open for lap swimming, restaurant dinner menus, and her retirement portfolio. *Should institutions of higher learning be allowed to use race as a factor in determining admissions? Why or why not?* She put those essays in her bag with dread about the work it would take to respond to them—to make comments, give feedback, give grades. Then she remembered that she'd forgotten about Hamish, had forgotten about him in the course of the day. Was that good or bad? She couldn't say.

Hot Springs

Eleven months out of twelve, the judge ignored being Jewish. Then Christmas slid into view, and for a while he was reminded of it. People who knew he was Jewish would say "Happy Hanukkah" in lieu of "Merry Christmas," and though he wanted to retort, "You don't understand; I'm an agnostic who has no more to do with Hanukkah than you do," he never answered anything of the sort. But still, Christmas forced his hand to the extent that December was his default vacation window. He and his wife, yearly, went somewhere balmy to wait out the season. Each November, they called their grown children—who had children of their own, Christmas trees, and colored lights—to repeat that December was a low-fare month for flights to sunny climes, and that it conduced to the judge's court schedule to mark off vacation time with annual consistency. Then, a few weeks later, away they went until just after New Year's, by which time Seattle had returned to normal in the sense that a nominal Jew like the judge could go for weeks without thinking about his birth religion.

But this year was different. Instead of winging off to a tropical locale, they were driving to Harrison Hot Springs in British Columbia, where Christmas was sure to be as omnipresent as it was at home, and—even more unusual—they had in tow the judge's parents, who were too elderly to handle airplanes anymore but who were great at long-distance travel on interstates because, he thought, of the steady, unchanging rhythm. His father, who was spindly and had a dire need for legroom, rode beside the judge in the front seat, oblivious, as always, to fields, towns, and mountains—to everything in the landscape—while his mother, wedged into the back beside the judge's wife, nattered on about herself: "I'm going with my quilt group on a quilting retreat during the third week of January, but I have to have a cyst removed from my neck the week before . . . walked downtown from his office and had lunch with . . . we went into the Old Navy store because of Dina's niece's daughter's birthday . . . tell you what Roberta said about me last . . . reminded me of me because she's so . . ." His father, the judge saw for the thousandth time in his life, hung on his wife's every word and seethed. Behind the wheel of his Civic Hybrid, driving toward Canada through midmorning rain, the judge seethed about her, too, mostly while displaying a cheery face, though sometimes the best he could do was to feign impassivity or act as if immersion in driving prevented him from nodding in the rearview mirror to acknowledge his mother when she demanded it. She'd say, leaning forward, "Don't you agree with me?" and he'd pretend, absorbed in interstate perils, that her question wasn't aimed at him.

"Your sisters have abandoned me," his mother insisted,

near Conway. "Don't you agree? Don't you think so, too?"
And he checked a side mirror, purse-lipped but provoked, then
changed lanes as if doing so was essential.

"Don't you agree? Your sisters? Hello?"

At which point he looked in his rearview mirror and said,
"I don't know."

"One is in South Africa and the other in Los Angeles," said
his mother. "Isn't that right?"

"Yes."

"So you agree with me."

He didn't answer. His mother said, "Well, that's why your
father and I had six kids. Oh boy, oh boy! We were sure busy,
weren't we, dear?"

"Yep," said his father.

They approached the border. By the time the judge had
answered the agent's questions, zipped up his window, and
rolled a little north, his mother had a fresh but familiar enthusiasm: "Handsome," she said. "That fella in the booth? My
God, he was so handsome!"

With a glance, the judge checked on his father, who said,
"From this point, the border, it's I think about an hour if—"

"You're changing the subject," his mother told him. "I
want you to comment on that handsome border fella. Didn't
you think he was handsome?"

"Yes."

"He could have been a model."

"Yes," his father repeated.

"A handsome, handsome man. Don't you think?"

Once again the judge feigned interest in the road, as if rain and traffic called for all of his attention. His father said, "I didn't really look."

"You didn't?" his mother asked. "He was unusual for a Canadian in that his skin was an olive tone. He might have been Greek or Italian—handsome! You know what I dislike about Canada?" she added. "They don't really have minorities here. They don't have the blacks and Hispanics like we do. Everyone here is lily-white. Everyone here is a WASP."

Time to speak up—he had to; this couldn't stand. He put a hand to his rearview mirror and said, "You're sitting next to a white Anglo-Saxon Protestant, Mom. My wife. Your daughter-in-law. For whom 'WASP' is a derogatory term."

His mother leaned forward and put a hand on his shoulder. " 'WASP' isn't derogatory," she said. "It's a description. It describes. Don't you know that?"

"No," he said. "I don't know it. 'WASP' is derogatory."

For the next hour—until they reached the hot springs—he regretted having broken a rule about his mother, his own three-part mantra: not worth it, you lose, keep your mouth shut.

There was snow on the ground at Harrison Hot Springs, or the remains of snow, a patch here or there, eroding to slush beneath the rain. Fortunately, they'd reserved ground-floor rooms with sliding glass doors, only steps from the adult pool, which boiled and steamed like a cauldron and at the moment steeped a dozen or so couples. Bathers came and went in white terry-cloth robes, padded along the covered walkways in zoris, toweled off in the frigid air, and knoodled in furtive corners. They were mostly Japanese—young couples with good haircuts, fashionable—engaged in misty giggling, teasing, and grappling while in easy reach of poolside drinks.

The judge, after putting on what his father called "swim trunks," prepared his own poolside drink—whiskey and water in an aluminum water bottle—and told his wife that, contrary to her repeated assertions on the matter, she looked fantastic in a bathing suit. "Right," she said, then in a well-knotted bathrobe left for the indoor round pool since it was the warmest on the premises at 104 degrees. The judge tried his drink, knocked on his parents' sliding door, waited for them to do the things they always did before they went out—use the bathroom, take pills, discuss footwear, discuss food—and then, because the patio was rain-slicked, he took his mother by one arm and his father by the other and led them to the steps, with sturdy rails, that gave access to the adult pool. Stoutly, on wide and dimpled legs, hands on her hips, his mother waded forward while his father, after a spate of preparatory heavy breathing and a few stated hesitations—"Oh boy, this is hot" . . . "Not my cup of tea"—immersed his drooping frame at last.

"Okay," said the judge. "I'll be right over there." He pointed. "In the pavilion."

"Go," said his mother. "The two of you deserve some lovey-dovey time."

The judge gave a little farewell wave and, carrying his water bottle, went into the pavilion and hung his robe on a peg. Finally—after a day of battles, hassles, and irritations—he parked himself, with a sigh, in the water beside his wife, whose cheeks looked flushed, even scalded. "Your mother's in extra-fine fettle," she observed. "On a roll. In her element. Long drive with captive audience."

"Sorry," said the judge.

"Of course she meant 'WASP' as an insult—obviously."

"It's true," said the judge. "But let's take the high road. There's no point getting into it with her."

He unscrewed his water bottle. The pool pavilion, lit by wall sconces against the winter dark outside the glass, was hushed and steamy and, like the adult pool outside, had a libidinous effect on bathers. Here, too, were couples at play. They made the judge feel pleased with his life, and in particular with his wife, who at fifty-four did look fantastic in a bathing suit. She was perennially a beauty—a shiksa, as his mother put it—shiny, golden, smooth-skinned, trim. The judge put an arm around her waist.

An hour later, showered and dressed, they sat with his parents by the resort's grand fireplace, the judge and his father in side-by-side armchairs and his wife and mother at one end of a sofa, where they paged through a coffee-table book called *Great Resorts and Lodges of North America*. Couples passed on their way to dinner, freshly groomed and neatly attired. On one side of the hearth stood a lit and tinseled Christmas tree, and on a nearby table a diorama depicted a snowy New England village circa 1925, decked out for Yule and inhabited, largely, by busy shoppers and frenetic children. Piped-in, if watered-down, carols played, and a swag of holly and winking lights traversed the mantel. The judge's father noticed none of it, preferring to rehearse, with the judge, their schedule: "Dinner at eight-fifteen, breakfast tomorrow at nine, around ten or ten-thirty this walk your mother keeps talking about so she can look into the shops and so forth, then—"

"You know," said the judge's mother, "it really drives me nuts when you do that all the time. Try to enjoy right now for once, will you? Stop talking about your calendar every second."

"It's a little after eight," his father replied. "Shouldn't we go now? Our reservation is for eight-fifteen."

Another couple approached. The man, bald in an exacting way, head shaved to a polished sheen, wore a plaid vest under a jacket stretched taut by a swell of hard belly fat. The woman, though silvered, didn't quite pull off patrician; her Scottish knitwear was elegant enough, but her makeup lacked subtlety. They were nevertheless, both of them, aspiring to baronial, which provoked the judge's mother: "Excuse me," she said as they stood with their backs to her, warming their hands and murmuring to one another. "Are you enjoying yourselves there by the fire?"

The man turned and said, "Why, yes, we are, thank you. Thank you for asking. Where are you from?"

The judge's mother turned a page of her coffee-table book and said, "No. I mean, what I mean is, would you move, please? Where you're standing right now you're blocking the fire. And we were here first."

The baron and the baroness glared, then stepped left in tandem. "Sorry," the judge said to them, only too aware that his mother looked and sounded like a Jew. "No big deal. We're heading off to dinner anyway. The fire's yours. Please, enjoy."

"The fire is communal," said his mother. "It's meant to

be shared. No one has the right to dominate it like that. It's everybody's."

"Forgive us," replied the baron, with thick irony. "You people have a nice evening if you can." And with that he saluted the judge's mother both combatively and dismissively, took his baroness by the elbow, and fled at a stately pace.

"And you, too," called the judge's mother after him. "Have a very, very nice evening!"

At eight-fifteen the judge's party sat for dinner in the Copper Room. Here, as in the lobby with its massive fireplace, Christmas was old-fashioned, fussy, and conspicuous—a tree, strung lights, garlands, seasonally accoutered staff, piped-in carols, gratis mulled wine, and a menu insert turned toward Yorkshire pudding and cranberry conserve. "Goyishe and hoity-toity," said his mother in a hushed tone, lest she goad into action the Copper Room's anti-Semites. "Just look at these prices! This isn't our world. This is for the goys, not us."

"Enjoy it," said the judge. "I'm paying for it."

"Listen to Mr. King of England," she said, studying her menu. "So ritzy, he's paying. Hey, for years, sonny, we paid for everything. For everything, everything, everything!"

"Exactly," said the judge. "So now it's my turn."

But inside he was steaming. His mother ruined everything; her mere presence was infuriating. He couldn't stand the sour odor of perfume or her gnomish face—like a fat, dried apple—or her witchlike head of hair or her squat, rotund figure. Actually, he couldn't stand anything about his mother—not at the moment, in the Copper Room, at Christmas. And he had to imagine his father felt this, too. In fact, he would have bet his entire fortune, however modest, that his father, moment by excruciating moment, experienced his wife of nearly six decades as a hellish, dogging, insufferable presence that, if you didn't do battle with it, however subtly, would drive you to despair.

The Copper Room, though subject to a dress code, was not so precious that it couldn't plate a roasted chicken, grilled filet of beef, or prime rib with mashed potatoes, which meant that the judge's parents could eat inside their accustomed parameters. The judge ordered wine and encouraged appetizers and salads, and, after dinner, desserts, which they ate while the Jones Boys warmed up their act. Before long, the first couples took to the sprung floor. One in particular was entertainingly good, and, despite gimpiness and years, danced ballroom with flair and swing with joie de vivre. It was cheering, even moving, but it veered toward schmaltz when the Jones Boys began what their front man called a "Christmas waltz in the Viennese style. The grand old Austrian style. One, two, and a-waaaaay we go!" he boomed.

Now the judge's father leaned in, as his mother had done earlier. Looking a little parboiled from his half-hour in the pool and his glass of wine, he said, "Sinatra used to do this song. Irony is, it was written by Sammy Cahn."

"Sammy Cahn!" exclaimed the judge's mother. "I'd completely forgotten about Sammy Cahn. 'Bei Mir Bist Du Schoen'—that was Sammy Cahn. It—"

"Sure," said the judge's father. "The Andrews Sisters." And now, off-key, he sang, over the Jones Boys:

> *I've tried to explain, bei mir bist du schoen*
> *So kiss me, and say you understand.*

"That's it!" the judge's mother cried, then kissed him, hard—mwah!—on the cheek. "You're sharp as a tack! And so, so handsome. Isn't your father handsome?" They drank to each other, and when the Jones Boys moved on to "Can't Take My Eyes Off of You," got up and approximated dancing.

"They're awful," the judge said, sitting back with his glass of port. "Look at them. They're embarrassing."

"No," replied his wife. "It's really, really cute. I love that. Look at them! All of a sudden they're having a good time! The hot spring's got them in a good mood."

"I don't get it," said the judge. "I don't get them at all."

"Don't try," said his wife, and slid her hand over his. "Let's dance!"

Krassavitseh

At dusk they were delivered by a driver named Jürgen to the five-star luxury Brandenburger Hof at Eislebener Strasse 14. It was not so much this hotel's location—near the Tiergarten and the Berlin University of the Arts—as it was its "exceptional service and taste" that had led the tour company to recommend it and then, on his approval, to reserve a double Comfort City room with twin beds and a sitting area. As soon as they were ensconced and organized—the geriatric toiletries arrayed by the bathroom sink—his father took hold of the remote control and tuned in CNN International. "Close enough," his father remarked, and fluffed his pillow. "I know this person—Amanpour." Then: "This is what the Krauts call sports? Nothing. I didn't get the scores."

"Germany doesn't own CNN, Dad."

"Can't even get the score of a ball game!"

"Okay, we'll go online, then," he said. "I can get you the *Seattle Times*."

"Puh."

But, at his father's behest, he got the scores anyway and then read aloud the names above obituaries, so that his father would know if, back at home, someone he knew had passed away since they'd boarded their plane for this trip to Berlin, where his father had lived as a child.

In the morning, they met their guide in the Brandenburger's lounge—otherwise known as the Quadriga—which was open-air and rife with perfect plants. The guide was a woman in her mid- or late twenties who was waiting for them with her coat over her arm, looking, he thought, poised but under strain. His first impression was of this blue elegance— a woman with enough learning to be generally troubled, but with enough youth, also, to enjoy herself. She appeared urbane and professional in caste. Her expression, her mien, her manner, her carriage—all of it, frankly, was not what he'd expected. He'd rather thought that Jewish Tours of Berlin would send them someone of substantially greater years, but, then, at his age—fifty-eight—he was perennially surprised that twentysomething people were able to do the jobs they did; so why not a tour guide, along with all the rest? Besides, this one seemed mature enough, courteous, considerate, amenable, intelligent. Her name, she said, was Erika Wolf, and her work, until recently, she gave them to understand, was at Berlin's German Historical Museum—"in walking distance of the Brandenburg Gate, eastward along Unter den Linden, which is a beautiful boulevard lined with lime trees"—though technically her employer had been the Federal Office for Central Services and Unresolved Property Issues. Erika Wolf had impeccable English with no hard edges or telltale Teutonic music. She wanted to know if they'd had their breakfast; if not, the hotel breakfast was very good. At this, his father opened his mouth. "Breakfast!" he said, looking at his watch. "For me, it's already six-fifteen p.m. because of the nine-hour time difference."

His father had dressed, on this April morning, in khakis, a sweater vest, and a button-down chambray: the travel outfit he'd bought the month before, when the two of them went to a mall for clothes and to pick up a rolling carry-on with swivel wheels, AARP five-star recommended but, even better, on sale. He'd also put on his comfortable walking shoes—the ones with room for custom orthotic inserts—and carried the lightweight nylon hooded parka he swore by as the ticket when it rained. Was it going to rain today? he asked. In Berlin, as they were "kicking around"? Erika Wolf smoothly fielded this query by pointing out that, though April was not the city's wettest month—that award went annually to June—one could never really be certain, and therefore it was a very good idea to have a raincoat such as his father was carrying. Or an umbrella, she added; there were three in her car.

Breakfast—he insisted his father eat breakfast and make every effort to time-zone adjust—was served by a Somali so conspicuously tall that his father, displaying his signature tactlessness, felt moved to tell her, "You could have blocked Michael Jordan." After that, they ate from tiered plates while Erika Wolf, not touching her tea, explained that this hotel was in the Prussian style and very close to the Kurfürstendamm—"our bleaker version of the Champs-Élysées"—and especially to the Kaiser Wilhelm Church—"actually," she said, "two distinct churches, the one what remains of the old church, most prominently its damaged spire, the other the four buildings of the new church, which has over twenty thousand stained-glass inlays."

His father, with food in his mouth, said, "Damaged how and when?"

"It was damaged in November of 1943, due to bombing."

"Too bad they didn't get the whole thing," replied his father.

Erika Wolf didn't answer. Instead she brought her hand to her mouth. After a while it moved to her throat, and then to her cheek, and then again to her mouth. The other hand joined it there.

They did, first, what they'd come to do—they made a tour of the Jewish quarter, where his father had lived in the thirties. Starting at the Rosa-Luxemburg-Platz, they followed Alte Schönhauser Strasse, Neue Schönhauser, and Rosenthaler Strasse, Erika Wolf judiciously providing facts and parceling out historical and architectural information. His father, a fast walker with a still-longish stride—someone who walked to get from A to B—seemed, on these streets, to shrink not just in stature but in irascibility. Zipped up tightly to the Adam's apple in his parka, he listened like a schoolboy to their guide.

On Grosse Hamburger Strasse they came to the Jewish School, where Erika Wolf stopped to look above the portico at head-to-head cherubs in sculptural relief and at a sign reading "Knabenschule der Jüdischen Gemeinde," meaning, she told them, "Jewish Community School for Boys."

His father craned his neck, scratched under his nostrils, pulled for a moment at the corners of his lips, and then, squinting, said, "This place I remember, exactly right here. This place is in my head."

He pointed a forefinger at a dark bust over the doorway— pointed as if in admonishment. "That guy scared me good," he said. "I didn't want to walk under that guy. Maybe you know what I'm talking about. Goofy things. Bad luck. Superstitions."

They looked for a while. Erika Wolf began to nod. "Yes," she said. "I can see it."

They went into the Alter Jüdischer Friedhof, no longer in use, for a long time not in use—in fact, all of the gravestones had been removed by the East Berlin Parks and Garden Department, so that now there was only what they were viewing together, a refurbished gravestone honoring Moses Mendelssohn and a sarcophagus filled with remains. There were, though, a number of *Stolpersteine*— "which translated directly means 'stumbling blocks' "—small brass plaques set in among the cobblestones inscribed with the names of deported Berliners. While his father stood pondering Mendelssohn's dates, he and Erika Wolf looked for *Stolpersteine*. When they were kneeling beside one, and out of his father's hearing range, he said, softly, "I'm sorry to pry. Are you Jewish?"

"No."

"Please don't take him personally."

"He has every right. I don't blame your father."

Her scarf was dangling so that its ends were on the cobble-stones, and her black hair partly hid her face. At that moment, she reminded him of his daughter, who was a pediatric epidemiologist—living right now in Sierra Leone—or, rather, he understood that Erika was a daughter, too, the daughter of a German father and mother who were glad, always, to hear from her or, even better, to have her come home, their Erika who'd grown up to be a wonderful person, sensitive, smart, capable, caring; Erika whom they sometimes worried about, partly because of her melancholy, and partly, and sim-ply, because she was their daughter and that was just what parents did—worry, automatically, even if they didn't want to; worry no matter how they tried not to; worry endlessly, or longer than they needed to; worry until, gradually, the tables turned, and their children began worrying about them.

"He means well," he told Erika. "He really, absolutely does."

Erika trapped her hair behind her ears, the better, he thought, to sustain a professional appearance. "Berlin," she said, "is full of ghosts."

Systematically, on foot, they covered the old Jewish quarter in the hope of finding on prompts for his father's memory on a par with the entrance to the boys' school. The Jewish quar-ter, though, was also the Scheunenviertel, a district dedicated to the shopping sensibilities of relatively young people with discretionary euros for Turkish throw pillows, cotton-hemp yoga pants, Swedish jeans, and whole-wheat apple strudel. In other words, the present obscured the past, and as they passed through the courtyards and walked the winding lanes, his father looked primarily flabbergasted by the thoroughness of his lack of recognition. A number of old walls were now canvases for street artists interested in depicting robots and dinosaurs, or in spray-painting gaudy and colorful collages; all of that obstructed his father's memory, as did substantial graffiti. Erika held out hope for the Neue Synagoge, and indeed his father recalled its golden dome and, inside, the height of its iron vaults, and sat for some time on a bench there, looking moved—blowing his nose, cleaning his glasses—but he could not remember anything else, and especially not the fire and pogrom of November 9, 1938. "We left before that," he told Erika, when she'd translated the plaque at the front of the building. "We left, I think, August, before it happened."

Erika put her hand over her mouth. His father moved his parka from one arm to the other. "August or maybe July," he said. "In a train we went to the Polish border. From there to Warsaw, and from there, I don't remember exactly, to Italy, to a ship, a steamship, a cruise ship, and we ended up in Shanghai, China—I know!—and that's where we passed the entire war, and you know who was there? Michael Blumenthal was there, who was treasury secretary under Jimmy Carter, and this guy I definitely remember very well, even though he was older than me. A smart guy, super, top-notch, A-one, and now Michael Blumenthal, he's somebody, he's famous."

He waited for Erika to say something about Shanghai, and when she didn't, he added, "They still have Jews in China to this day. There's this guy I know, Goldschag, he stayed, never left, but he also has a place in London."

They moved on, but couldn't find the house he'd lived in,

though he remembered that it had been on a narrow lane—a lane now maybe gone altogether. Later, he remembered throwing rocks in the Spree and, with more clarity, its high, noxious smell on a day when it was raining "like no tomorrow." In the hope of inciting more such memories, they walked the riverside promenade from Monbijou Park to Tucholsky Strasse, where his father said, "There were two boys I knew that we used to play a game like kickball together, and I remember that one of them had this port-wine stain"—he patted his right cheek from his ear to his chin—"right here, all red, all inflamed, *huge,* and once, I teased him, I made fun of him a little, and the guy, he wouldn't talk to me for *weeks.*"

His father wanted just ice cream for lunch, so Erika drove them in her clean, small sedan for gelato near the Berliner Grossmarkt. There they discussed their afternoon options, deciding, first, on the Otto Weidt Museum, which honored a blind businessman who'd saved Jews. After that they went to the Babelplatz to see the vault of empty bookcases entombed beneath cobbles but visible through glass. Then it was on to the Topography of Terror—on the site of the former Gestapo and SS headquarters—and finally, near dusk, to the memorial at Grunewald, with its "186 cast steel plates, each with the date of transport, the number of deportees, the point of departure, and the destination of Jews who were sent from here to the death camps." Throughout all of this, whenever he had the chance—that is, when his father was out of hearing range—he asked their tour guide personal questions without, he hoped, an invasive cast; he pressed her for basic biographical data, and when he had that, for its clarification: Erika was from Blankenese; where was that? What sort of industry was primary there? What sort of landscape—mountains, plains? Erika had gone to university in Freiburg—how was that? The classes and professors? Degrees in what, and when, and why? Her former work at the German Historical Museum—specifically what work, its nature and purpose? Not, though, do you live with somebody, or where do you live, or are you married or attached? "Do you enjoy your work as a tour guide?" was all right, but not "Why did you leave the museum?" or "What do you do with your free time?"

Gradually, Erika emerged as a person. Blankenese was a wealthy suburb of Hamburg, the epicenter of German banking. Her father was the founder of a real-estate company with international franchises and regional offices in Hong Kong and Los Angeles. Her mother worked for a company in the promotional-products market as a full-time consultant to customers. Erika had a brother in London studying international relations, and another in Heidelberg who was a media photographer. At Freiburg she'd studied comparative history of the modern age and library science. She'd come to Berlin for an internship at the historical museum, and also to take six terms of museum studies at the Berlin University of Applied Sciences. At first she'd been interested in the conservation of historical monuments, but in time she'd turned to collections care, and this was the sort of work she'd done until, of late, deciding on a different course—one she didn't articulate, nor did he press her on it. But he did ask—he said he was curious—about the government bureaucracy she'd mentioned that morning, the "Office of Property Issues."

It was the Federal Office for Central Services and Unresolved Property Issues. This was the office whose purpose, she explained, was to provide restitution to victims of the Nazis, or compensation for their losses. Her work at the museum had been primarily concerned with "registering stolen cultural property"—specifically, works of art. She spent her time traveling paper trails in order to determine legitimate ownership of the artwork held in the museum's collection, so that it might be returned to its rightful owners or, where there were none living—almost always the case—their heirs.

It was nearly dark and had gotten so frigid that his father had his hood over his head and his hands in his parka pockets. Yet still he moved down the railroad tracks, reading about deportations from Grunewald. Above him, on the platform, he and Erika kept watch like guardian angels. She'd wrapped her scarf from right to left across her throat and pulled on a pair of wool mittens. She was, he noticed, shivering a little. Her narrow shoulders were high and hunched. A feeling of tenderness came over him, to think that she was suffering from the cold.

The next morning, they went to Sachsenhausen beneath a pale and cloudless sky. He found Sachsenhausen queasily unbearable, and did and did not want to see the crematorium, the medical-postmortem table, the execution trench, the pathology block, or any of the rest of it; he didn't want to look but felt he must at the hill of gold teeth, the medical-crimes cellar, and Room 51 of Barrack RII, where children were—could it be?—tortured. Who tortured children? Who *could* torture children? The answer was in the T-building, formerly the staff building. Here were photographs of the people who'd done it. He looked at these alongside his father, who appeared, he thought, to have a stronger stomach for it all, which, he surmised, stemmed from his advanced years, but he couldn't be sure that this was the reason; maybe he himself was just weak in the knees when it came to this grisly and unthinkable place's communicating a truth he'd thought he'd known.

They drove toward Wannsee while his father, incensed, offered a familiar litany. "The last thing I'd do is buy anything German—not a car, nothing, not even a pencil, and if this guy next to me hadn't popped for my ticket, I never would have flown on Lufthansa." Next he told Erika that he hated Volkswagens, and that "when my wife, who's gone, got me a Braun shaver, I traded it in for a Schick." Also, when he watched the Olympics on television, he hoped all the Germans would come in "dead last," and when he saw them on the news drinking beer at Oktoberfest, he gave his television the finger. Germany didn't have any artists or writers because Germans lacked souls. Their so-called philosophers were fascist pigs. And they were such thorough dummkopfs they kicked out the Jews, who then went ahead and invented the bomb, "but in America," said his father. "What idiots!"

Erika remained silent in the face of this harangue, as if she had steeled herself to it. Today she wore a different coat— long, belted, and double-breasted—and had captured her hair in a loose ballerina bun, out of which splayed a spiral of loose ends; she drove, always, with two hands on the wheel and with her seat pulled close to the pedals. All of this made her look vulnerable somehow, and also, he thought, a little undernourished—Erika appeared, to his eyes, gray and frail, too small for her coat and overbundled for the weather, which at noon, as they passed through leafy forest, was sunny and fair, as if the world were blown clean—no sign, anywhere, of the impossible past, of a past that couldn't really have happened.

At Wannsee they visited the villa above the lake where, as Erika explained—standing by the roses on the circular drive—"the Final Solution was planned, in 1942, by fifteen Germans, including Adolf Eichmann, who was only thirty-five at the time."

"And do you know what became of Eichmann?" asked his father. "For eight years he was a free man in Argentina, until the Mossad threw him into the back of a car, and then they put that pig on the stand and hung him by the neck in Israel. And too bad they couldn't hang him twice!"

They went in. They stood in the conference room—actually a dining room—where the plans had been hatched. The sunroom looked out onto yet more roses. The museum was divided into fourteen sections, and in each his father bent over display cases, zeroing in on the fine print intently for two hours and forty-five minutes.

It was invasive, really, but in the circular foyer—where they waited while his father took his time in the toilet—he asked for forgiveness in prelude to his question, then said that her former work sounded interesting but that he had to wonder why she had quit, and also, what came next.

Erika, with her car keys in hand, belted her coat a little tighter. "Of course, you can ask me anything," she said. "For me, the next step is law school."

"I'm a retired attorney," he told her. "Mostly my practice was pretty mundane, but at any rate I applaud your choice. Although I should warn you that the law is all-consuming and that a lawyer almost never stops. You're either all the way in or you're out."

"Yes," said Erika. "And as for the Deutsches Historisches Museum, I found myself very frustrated there. So much work I put in for them to establish who owned the Friedrich Hagedorn or the Grosz or the Knaus or the Diefenbach, and then their lawyers establish doubt so the museum can keep these works in its collection. What I made clear, they clouded over. And they were very, very good at it," she added.

The *Herren* door opened and his father stepped out. "One thing about this country," he said. "I gotta give 'em credit for their bathrooms."

Back in Berlin they visited Café Einstein, because his father needed to rest for a bit, and because, in the wind that had stirred in the afternoon, the city had begun to grow cold again. Inside the café, however, it was warm—warm to the point of languorously cozy—and bustling, too, with lingering coffee drinkers, and with people eating large wedges of cheesecake and the specialty of the house, apple strudel. The strudel, its smell, awakened in his father a memory of strudel, and so Erika ordered it for him with a cup of drip coffee, and a piece of cheesecake with a cappuccino—why not?—but only, for herself, black tea, since she didn't want to eat, even though he said it would be on him in the paternal tone he'd deployed toward her since the evening before, when, in the cold, at dusk, at Grunewald, they'd stood on the platform keeping watch over his father.

Refreshed, they walked to the Memorial to the Murdered Jews of Europe, a battery of "stelae" in the middle of Berlin that rose like concrete tombs or chimneys, faceless and without inscription. These were arranged in claustrophobic rows that dipped into increasing darkness, and into which his father disappeared. Here, in the low light of midafternoon, with their faces flushed by exertion and flirtation, a group of schoolchildren, oblivious to history, were playing tag among the stelae. Erika said sternly, "This is not right—where is their teacher?" and "Germans simply go on with their lives as if they had every right to be ignorant," and "We don't have the right to be eating our strudel, and there should not be Somali women serving us at tables. I'm sorry, you don't do what Germans did and just go on always talking about your guilt and building more museums and memorials. What you do is, you do your own dishes, and also you give every single thing back, all of the linens and the townhouses stolen, you give back the strudel, you teach your children to give back the strudel, this is the punishment, and we should serve the long sentence, not a single German should be indifferent, and let those who say I am guilt-obsessed tell it to the murdered six million."

"Agreed," he said. "But they're dead."

They stood beside a row of trees, near where the children were being called to their school bus; his father was nowhere to be seen. Erika, frowning, said, "Believe me, I know all the counterarguments. I've read the Goldhagen, the Christopher Browning, the Karl Jaspers, the Carl Jung, and in school of course *The Burden of Guilt,* which is a famous book here in Germany." Now she frowned at two boys running past. "Today," she said, "there are all these people my age who are conflicted about joining German society because then they can no longer say to themselves, 'I am a child, and a child is not responsible.' That is something I won't do," she said. "Everybody has to grow up."

In the wind and the gradually failing light, she looked to him, though wan, committed—committed in the sense of idealists he'd known, like his daughter, the pediatric epidemiologist. He himself had just made money. Not that money was bad. You could only give it away if you had it. But this Erika Wolf, from a city of German banks, from a family of rich Germans, wanted something else from life.

For three more days they made pilgrimages together, always on behalf of his father. They drove to Potsdam and toured the Cecilienhof Palace, where Stalin, Churchill, and Truman carved up Europe—something, his father said, they heard about in Shanghai a month after it happened. On a morning of rain, they visited Berlin's Jewish Museum, which was so enormous and complicated, and so perplexing and unnerving, that they ended up spending nearly the day there, after which his father said he'd like to visit cemeteries. On their last day, then, Erika drove them to Weissensee, where she called their attention to the Art Nouveau mausoleums and to a plaque commemorating Herbert Baum, who, she explained, "was a prominent member of the resistance to Nazism and somebody I wrote on at university." There was another cemetery on Heerstrasse, close to the Olympic Park, and a third on Schönhauser Allee that, beside its hoary wrought-iron gates, had a lapidarium displaying damaged headstones. He and his father wore the mandatory *Schädeldecke* to wander, in silence, among the graves.

At their farewell in front of the Brandenburger Hof, his father tried to give Erika a hundred euros—"a little something, not much, a gratuity"—but she wore him down about taking it from him until his father stuffed it back in his wallet, shrugged, and said, "Have it your way." For his own part, he shook their tour guide's hand with a formal distance he didn't really feel; what he wanted was to hug her affectionately, but he didn't feel right about doing that; for him, a lot of rules were in play that he did not want to abridge. He said, "It has certainly been a very great pleasure to spend these last five days with you, and my father and I both thank you from the bottoms of our hearts for everything you've done. We mean it."

At this, his father hit him on the shoulder. "What kind of a goodbye is *that*?" he asked. "Come here," he said to Erika, and hugged her.

They were in the air, just taking off, when his father observed, looking out the window, "I'll never see Berlin again, you can bet your bottom dollar on that!"

Hours later, over the Atlantic, his father leaned in close to say, "That was a very nice girl we had. With a very nice *tuchus,* by the way."

He had to laugh. His father touched his arm. "Wolf," said his father. "Erika Wolf. You went to temple with kids named Wolf. You gotta remember—Danny Wolf? Danny, I think, was the one your age. His mother and father I knew a long time. His father was the one who screwed everything up when he worked for the city or the county in the sixties and almost had to serve jail time." Now his father put a hand to his chin. The plane bumped a little, into the wind. "I think Danny is the one who ended up a lawyer. *One* of the boys is a lawyer, I know that. I can't keep the Wolfs straight. There's so many Wolfs. You look in the phone book and there's hundreds of these Wolfs that used to be there, coming to temple. Anyway, that company didn't send a goy, *baruch HaShem.* We got the real deal—a Wolf—in Berlin! And this one such a *krassavitseh*—which in the old days we called a first-class Jewish woman, top of the line, someone to be *respected.* A *krassavitseh* toured us around Berlin! A Jewish woman showed us Berlin!"

Shadow

He went in for tests that revealed changes in his frontal lobes. A battery of interviews yielded the conclusion that his short-term memory had declined. His ability to act serially was compromised, and he'd lost what a doctor called "executive function." All of this within three months of retiring—not what he'd had in mind.

He and his wife took a cruise after that. Endless eating, talking, and milling. Disgruntled, and determined not to participate, he looked for corners in which to read magazines. At night, he placated his wife with a little dancing. One evening, an entertainer called three couples to a stage, including them, because his wife raised both hands. In front of everyone, so everyone could laugh, the entertainer accosted them with intimate questions, but he wouldn't be pulled into innuendo, he wouldn't be pulled into anything for idiots, and, most of all, he would scrupulously say the right thing, to keep his wife from his throat. Yet the cruise ended on a bad note anyway, with his wife upset because, obviously, he loathed cruising.

Retirement wasn't going very well. But then his young-est son called, after eight long months, saying, "Hey, it's me. Remember me?"

He panicked. He had no words. This son was so flaky, hard to fathom, unsteady. In his mid-twenties, he'd floated with a backpack. Then he became a war correspondent in Bosnia. They didn't hear from him much after that, and when they did, he was far away. He married a Bosnian, then a Kenyan—possibly he was still married to both. If he had kids, they didn't know about it. They'd pinned him down, finally, in 2002, by flying to Nairobi and getting a room at the Hil-ton, where they'd confronted him by a pool. He looked ter-rible. Some disease or other had ravaged his complexion, but he didn't want to go into the details. They suspected he had AIDS. The boy's mother made a desperate push to fathom her son, but the most he would say was that he loved his work and enjoyed his travels. He didn't characterize it exactly that way, but it was what they told his siblings by telephone from their room in the Hilton, in an effort to paint the picture with at least a few bright colors. Actually, the Africa trip was exhaust-ing and depressing, but between himself and his son . . . was the word "affinity"? He felt an affinity for this son of his, yes. He cheered for him. Defended him against his mother. And, with surprising frequency, he dreamed about him.

Usually when his son called he sounded blurry and distant, but this time he might have been right next door, that's how normal the connection was. It was good the boy's mother was out of the house—having told him not to touch anything, to wait until she got back from Target—because otherwise he would have had to yell for her right now so she could get on the line and take over. "Hey," he said, "it's you! Great!"

And it was great. Whereas his other three kids had been born in quick succession when he was too young to know what was going on, this one had arrived after a hiatus of ten years, when he was better established in his line of work—law— better able to support his family, and generally wiser and more mature—that is, mature enough to know that life passes by while you keep your nose to the grindstone. Was that trite? He didn't care if it was trite. He was a sentimentalist—he knew that about himself. He was sentimental about this boy, his baby, who'd been an independent soul from the start.

His son explained that he was in Alabama, but only for a few days before flying to Cameroon. "Alabama?" he asked. "Isn't that where those Jewish boys were killed? In June of '64? One named Schwimmer? Along with a black individual as well? It was in that movie *Mississippi Burning*. They nominated it for the Academy Award, but *Driving Miss Daisy* beat it out."

"No. I don't think so."

"You were born in '64. Three days after Johnson drubbed Goldwater. It was terrible timing. I was in the middle of a trial. I had to juggle so many things...." He became aware that he was speaking nonsense and said, "What are you doing in Alabama?"

"Interviewing people. But—do you want to come down, Dad, and pay me a visit? We could visit a few of the sites."

"The sites?"

"Where things happened. During the civil rights movement. We could go to Montgomery and Birmingham. You get a ticket into Atlanta, and I'll drive over there and pick you up."

Actually, that sounded good. Most travel sounded bad, but that sounded good. After all, civil rights was up his alley. In his early thirties, he'd been the county chair of the Anti-Defamation League, and in his mid-thirties, the president of his B'nai B'rith chapter—both groups interested in civil rights. Yes, this was his cup of tea, except that it meant going to the South, where, as a child, he'd decided never to go because of anti-Semitism. He took seriously the tales of people who were stopped by sheriffs because a taillight was out, then thrown in a backwater jail until they'd paid an absurdly hefty fine and endured right-wing abuse. No, it wasn't worth the risk, visiting the South. The South wasn't for Jews. Besides, there were things on his calendar—two doctor appointments, his mother's yarhzeit, a play he'd agreed to go to with his wife—and it seemed to him he should get past all those things before adding anything more. How had he ever had time to work? He couldn't figure out how he'd gotten it all done. Alabama? That couldn't happen. How could it happen? What would his wife say? She would say that he wanted to go to Alabama but not on a cruise. Just bringing up Alabama, a broaching, a mention, would rock her boat, throw her for a loop. And anyway, he was on a picky-eating regimen, because if he didn't eat the right food the bathroom was impossible. Would they have what he needed in Alabama? Not only that, but since 9/11 you couldn't take cuticle scissors or razors on an airplane. And even if you did get your razors through, it was difficult to shave in a hotel mirror, because the lights weren't right, or the water wasn't hot enough, or the sink was too far back or too shallow or had a complicated stopper. So what should he say now? Into the phone? He'd been silent for so long, without an answer for his son, it could reasonably corroborate the dementia diagnosis. Had one of his other kids contacted this one to say that their father was enfeebled by dementia and could use a pick-me-up invitation to Alabama? Did the kids sneak around behind his back that way? Probably they did, in a silent conspiracy—although, he knew, they were well intended. But he didn't want to be a charity case. He didn't think he needed their concern or assistance. He was a man who still knew how to operate in the world. So what was wrong with everybody? Talking about him as if he was a baby, talking about him to his face that way, talking about him as if he weren't there, about his driving, clothing, eating habits, etc. . . . . "Hey," he said to his son, "you know what I think? I think that sounds good. Civil rights tourism in Alabama—fantastic! Great! Let me check on it with your mother."

"Right," said his son. "Check with her and call me back."

She came home from Target. He checked on it with her, but she berated him for even thinking about it. "You're not going to Alabama," she said. "How would you find your way around?"

"You're treating me like a child again," he said, throwing up his hands. "Until a few months ago, I was downtown every day, Monday through Friday, eight until six, doing all sorts of things on my own."

"It's mean of him to invite you and not me," she replied.

"He doesn't want to see me. I'm his mother, and he doesn't want to see me."

"It's wrong," he agreed. "After all, you're his mother." And then, lawyer that he was, or had been for a long time, he said that it was important to connect with their son and that their son had laid down his terms for a connection, so what choice did they have? He had to go. She caved after that and—reluctantly, full of warnings—went to her computer and bought his tickets, which included a plane change in St. Louis. Next, finding their son's number on the caller ID, she called him and, with hurt in her voice, left a message with the flight numbers. "Meet him in baggage claim," she added, and hung up.

His oldest son, a lawyer, too, drove him, the next day, to Sea-Tac Airport. En route in this son's brand new "Smart Car," he wished his son wouldn't tool along in the slow lane. Nevertheless, they were 105 minutes early, which should have given him plenty of extra time, except that his son thought it necessary to park, roll his suitcase for him, and read signs the way you'd read them to a three-year-old, instead of, more efficiently, just dropping him at Departures. What could he do? His son handled the seat assignments, boarding passes, and baggage tag. He led the way down the concourse. They hugged, and then they were separated by Security. He took his place at the end of a long line that very quickly got longer behind him. His son waved and receded, and then he was alone. He waited his turn, but when his turn came, he'd failed to understand about his shoes and belt and had to wrestle, in a time crunch, with these wardrobe items. After some trouble

with his shoelaces (he'd double-knotted that morning, at his
wife's insistence), he was told to empty his pockets into what
looked like a dog bowl, and in so doing spilled change. A lucky
thing next—in a switch from what was normal, he made it
through the metal detector without a hitch. Then back to normal: the X-ray machine picked out his razors, so he had to wait
while a security guard unpacked and examined everything in
his bag. In the end, he was admonished for his razors, and lost
his razors, and had to hear the rule about razors, which he
already knew but had hoped to circumvent, and now feigned
surprise at. "Really?" he said to his tormentor, innocently. "Is
that true?"

He got through, eventually, but before anything else could
happen, he remembered his medications, and that swallow-
ing them demanded water. A bottle of water was $3.50, so,
instead of spending such an outrageous sum, he went to a
coffee shop—he thought, creatively—to ask for a free cup he
could use at a drinking fountain. There was a line for coffee.
He wanted to ignore it and just ask for a cup—play the geriatric card, maybe—but he didn't feel comfortable as a line cutter.
So he waited, uneasily, since he hadn't found his gate yet. At
last he got the cup from the hand of a girl who was surpris-
ingly polite, efficient, and clearheaded. Then he looked for a
drinking fountain, but when he found one, it turned out that
his medications weren't in his carry-on bag, no matter how
many times he looked for them. "It's just as well," he thought.
"Travel stuffs up my system enough without pills making
things worse."

Cup in hand, he searched for his gate. "You see, no problem," he thought, on finding it—he wasn't a child, he didn't have "dementia." He felt in his jacket for his boarding passes—check. He looked at them, then at the gate number. He read the display board behind the check-in counter. In a while, it dawned on him that this wasn't the right gate—that this was the gate he should be at in St. Louis, in order to board for his connecting flight to Atlanta, where the plan was to meet his son. How could that be? He stood in another line, in order to explain himself to the girl at the check-in desk, who, though preoccupied with something on her computer screen, took his boarding passes and corroborated his conclusion: indeed, he'd come to the wrong gate and, even worse, was in the wrong terminal. He would have to go back the way he'd come and follow the signs to a tram.

He hurried off. This was why you came early—this was exactly why you came early—this was why you drove efficiently and didn't waste time. This was why you didn't muddy the waters with two boarding passes. Why didn't other people get basic principles? What would he do if he missed his plane? He found the tram but, on board, the announcements for stops were in multiple languages. English came first, but then a lengthy progression of gobbledygook intervened, such that, by the time all was said and done, no one could have reasonably remembered what the English was about. At any rate, the tram stopped, the doors opened, and since no one got out, neither did he. Which was a mistake, because the only stop after that was at baggage claim.

Now he'd really muffed it. He knew that. He wasn't going to kid himself—he'd muffed it, as his wife had predicted. He was going to have to go through Security again, start over at step one, show his ID, and take off his shoes—his shoes, which he'd neglected to double-knot after his last bout with Security, so that one was untied. "Oh well," he thought. "Why tie it now, when I'll only have to take it off again in a few minutes?"

He went into action, following signs to Security, but then, seeing a kiosk marked "Traveler's Aid," got sidetracked. It seemed to him that what he needed at this point was a dispensation; he believed that if he could get someone to understand, they would whisk him past the checkpoints and assorted aggravations that stood between him and his gate. The someone at the kiosk—his potential savior, his miracle worker—turned out to be an Asian woman who wore the same expression his wife wore when he explained similar things to her—when he explained how a sequence of events hadn't gone right through no fault of his own. It was a face that said he was half a man. It was an expression that hit him in his octogenarian kishkes. "You're not going to bypass Security," she said. "If I were you, I'd get a move on."

He got a move on. There were twenty-seven minutes left. A lot of travelers might not panic about having twenty-seven minutes to make a plane, but at his age, he was more aware than they were of things that could go wrong. Further calamities might be waiting for him down the road. Sometimes bad luck was inevitable and things came together in exactly the wrong way—not very often, but it happened. Maybe this was one of those times. Maybe the best move was to give up now and, from a pay phone, call his wife for a ride home. But, no, he didn't want to do that.

At Security, he skipped the line and tried to explain that he was about to miss his flight, but when he started in on the narrative he'd mapped out, the guard he was appealing to—a caramel-colored giant in a very clean uniform—pointed to the end of the line. "I'm eighty," he pleaded. "Please. Have compassion."

"Compassion," said the guard, flatly, in a rich baritone. "Back of the line, sir." He pointed, then examined another traveler's ID.

"Please—isn't there a special arrangement for someone late? I'm very, very late for my plane."

But the guard didn't answer. Instead, he motioned the next traveler forward, took the next picture ID and boarding pass, looked up, glared, said, "I'm counting to ten," and, while examining documents again, began counting.

"Come on, now," he said. "Have some understanding. Do you think I look like Osama bin Laden? Do you think I'm going to blow up my own plane? Let's be reasonable for a moment here. I'm asking you to be a reasonable human being. I have a plane to make that I don't want to miss. I'm traveling to St. Louis, and in St. Louis, after waiting for fifty-five minutes in the airport, I'm changing planes for Atlanta so I can see my beloved son, who I haven't seen in six and a half years, six years and five months—a long time. Do you have a son, sir? My son—does that make sense to you? I'm asking you to be decent about this, good and decent in your heart."

"Ten," said the guard. "And now, since I'm good and decent in my heart, I'm going to give you one more chance to go to the back of the line, sir. Federal rules."

Such *mishegas*. People were either too young or too dumb to understand what was obvious. Everything now was run by idiots. "Please," he yelled. "This is terrible!" He stepped up with his boarding pass and picture ID and shoved them in front of the guard.

But then another guard was at his elbow. In fact, he was taking his elbow, not roughly—but nevertheless. A man about the age he'd been when his youngest son was born. "Come with me, sir," he said. "Come on, come with me, let's go."

"If you could just get me through Security," he replied, "that would be the right thing to do."

But he could feel that this new guard didn't mean to guide him toward the metal detector and X-ray machine. No, this new guard, already, was taking him in the opposite direction, and now he understood: he'd missed his flight.

His son the lawyer looked neither distressed nor surprised on taking delivery of his father. He rolled the suitcase again, negotiated the concourse, skybridge, and escalators, spoke soothing words about the situation, and then, after leaving the airport, drove in the slow lane with jazz music on softly and—breaking the law—made two cell-phone calls, one to report on their progress to his mother, the other to leave a message to the same effect for his brother in Atlanta. His primary comment on things was "It's really too bad," offered a half-dozen times.

The traffic was horrendous. "This isn't how it used to be," he thought, "in my day." He saw his building, or what used to be his building, as they inched through downtown, where he had another thought—that he wanted to be going downtown every day again; that retirement was a nightmare. "I miss working," he confided to his son, who replied that for him, work had never been fun. This made him think of something. "In 1951," he said, "they told your grandmother she had cancer. It was here." He indicated his intestines. "Terrible cancer. She was so-so for eighteen months, but then downhill. They couldn't do anything for her. Nuts. I was twenty at the time."

"Yes," said his son.

"Twenty and five months. I'd already met your mother. There were two things going on for me right then. Number one, your mother. I didn't date before that. Sometimes at the Sammy house, one date, but never a second. I was terrible with girls. Then—your mother. Number two, at university, I wasn't sure what to do. In high school, I'd really enjoyed writing for the school newspaper, but it was a toss-up for me, journalist or lawyer. My mother was very wise about this. She was the key person, really, in our family. My father was out of it compared to her—he was easygoing, everybody loved him, but my mother ran things. She was orderly, my mother, she ran a tight ship. She was absolutely perfect in every regard and a wonderful lady, widely respected. To me, every year I live past forty-nine, which is how old she was when she died—that's a bonus I don't deserve. I try to remember that, but I don't always succeed. I'm not perfect."

"She probably wasn't perfect, either, Dad. Not really."

They were plodding along in the slow lane behind a truck. They couldn't see a thing, but his son didn't seem to mind.

He just kept driving, with ample braking room, and his jazz music softly playing.

"No—not perfect. But she gave me good advice. On her deathbed. She didn't have long to live. In fact, we reset our wedding date for April 21 because my mother wanted to see me married—I knew that, so we moved up the date."

"Yes, I know. That was good of you."

He touched his son's arm. Here was the punch line, and he didn't want his son to miss it. He said, "She told me, 'The way I see it, if you want to be a journalist, you can always be a journalist, but if you want to be a lawyer, you need to go to law school. You have to have that sheepskin on your wall.' And that was right. That was very wise. That had an impact on my entire life. The way my mother handled that was perfect."

His son got off at 65th when he should have gotten off at 73rd and taken a quick right before the tunnel. Why didn't he know that? After all these years? The way to go? The right way to get home? Still, one way or another, he was heading home, and it was a relief, in a way, that this was so. Because the whole thing had really been one big hassle. Easier, more sensible, to stay home, where he belonged. Besides, his system wasn't right away from home—not that it was right when he was at home, either. Always plugged up, stuck, that was him, here or there, at home or elsewhere. Well, there were pros and cons to every choice, ups and downs, pluses and minuses—a plus was that his wife would be happy with how things turned out, vindicated by his airport confusion, and glad to have him back in her fold, where, as she put it to their kids sometimes, she could "keep an eye on him." Fine, if that gave her satisfaction, but, on the minus side, he'd missed his son, the world traveler and independent journalist. Maybe from now on he'd see him just in dreams, and hear his voice exclusively on the telephone, at long intervals—obscured, disembodied. Would he even know him if he saw him again? Would he recognize his son for who he was?

Photograph

Hutchinson's son died in October. He and the captain of the gillnetter *Fearless* went down in sixty-five-knot winds near a place called Cape Fox. The captain survived, but Paul was lost. The news came to Hutchinson and his wife in the form of a phone call followed by a fax from the Coast Guard station in Ketchikan, Alaska.

The day the news arrived, Hutchinson had gone duck hunting and shot his limit by eleven-thirty. While his wife was speaking to the Coast Guard petty officer, Hutchinson was on the road between Vantage and Ellensburg and feeling keenly the pleasure of his existence—three greenheads and a mallard hen in the cooler behind him, his dog asleep with her head on her paws, a thermos of coffee wedged against the dashboard, the heat and the radio on. While he rolled through Rye Pass and into the Ellensburg Valley, his wife read the fax five times. Later, she looked at photo albums, starting with Paul as a baby. She found a lot of photos from hunting expeditions, including one of Paul holding a duck by the neck and smiling, stiffly, for the camera.

While his wife grieved over photos, Hutchinson ate a midday breakfast at the Sportman's Café in Cle Elum. There were maybe a dozen other males present—smoking, drinking, staring at a screen—and Hutchinson found that the atmosphere of the place undercut the joie de vivre that had been growing in him all morning. He'd taken a booth and, with the sports section propped against a napkin dispenser, eaten two eggs, hash browns, sausage, and sourdough toast spread with jam. Now, six weeks later, it was the last decent meal he could remember eating. He remembered that after it he'd driven through Snoqualmie Pass feeling certain it was a good thing to arrive home early. He would have ample time to get things put away. He would draw, pluck, and roast two of his ducks.

His wife met him at the door with the news, and Hutchinson, not believing it for a moment, hurried into the house to read the death notice from the Coast Guard.

They were eating dinner. There was no such thing as dinner. Hutchinson and his wife had both stopped cooking. She lived on slices of cheese.

"You can say that," said Hutchinson. "You can accuse me of that. But I don't have to think it's fair."

He leaned against the stove. In one hand he held a spoon, in the other a soup pot. His wife was at the table with a box of corn flakes in front of her. She wasn't eating, either.

"I'm guilty," said Hutchinson. "Of course I'm guilty. But I blame you, too, Laura. We blame each other."

She didn't look at him. She was very much this sort of woman, and he had always known that. She could be cold—

she went cold when she got angry. "What you say is true," he said. "But you babied him."

"Twist and turn," she replied, and left the kitchen.

He stayed by the stove, insisting to himself that it was equally her fault for—for what exactly? Could he really say that babying a kid just made him press all the harder? He could say that. And hadn't he warned her? When he heard her coming back down the hall, he turned toward the burners. "I think I want you to leave," she said. "I can't stand the sight of you anymore."

The next week, he gave her to understand over the telephone that he was entitled to see his daughter, who was home for the weekend. Laura told him to come on Saturday. She said that the captain of the *Fearless* had called. He, too, would come on Saturday—Saturday night, for dinner.

The captain of the *Fearless* was standing in the living room with a bourbon and water when Hutchinson showed up. "I'm Bob Pomeroy," he said. "Your son was a great guy."

He didn't look like a fisherman. Wire-rimmed glasses sat cock-eyed on his nose. He blinked often. His lips were cracked.

They sat in the dining room. Hutchinson's daughter had changed her hairstyle: a pageboy, tinted red. She wore a smock and knickers. Her glasses hung from a chain around her neck. When Bob Pomeroy asked her politely about college, she said she'd recently changed her major from art with a focus on photomedia to art with a focus on visual communication design. Hutchinson hadn't known about that.

When the food was on the table, Bob Pomeroy shook his

head and pressed his glasses against his nose with a dry, fissured forefinger. "I'm sorry," he said. "I don't think I can eat."

He leaned toward Hutchinson across the table. "I'm in knots," he said. "I better just lay it all out here. I have to tell you what happened," he said. "I feel I owe you that."

The food grew cold. No one touched anything. Bob Pomeroy pushed his plate away, slid a map from the inner pocket of his jacket, unfolded it, and turned it in Hutchinson's direction. "Some background," he said, "and context."

The *Fearless* was a salmon boat, he explained, geared to gillnet or to troll, depending. For the last two seasons he'd fished with his girlfriend. This year they'd run the Inside Passage in mid-April, trolled from the Pedro Grounds to Cape Chirikof through mid-June, then worked the net through the height of the Alaskan summer. Basically, all of that was a bust—three months of headaches. They went through a lot of foul, nasty weather, doubling and even tripling up a lot of lines that chafed through in a week's time. A good net sank, and they passed too many hours tied up to floats, waiting for better conditions. Then, in mid-July, Bob's girlfriend left him. She got off the boat at Port Chilkoot, south of Haines, and refused to come back on board. The result was that Bob had to find a new deckhand, which he did by running up to Skagway. In a tourist saloon, he turned up Paul, who was nineteen and a half and weighed 210 pounds—precisely at that juncture in his earthly existence when he was capable of pushing his body hardest. He seemed eager. He and a friend had driven north from Bellingham in a truck with a mounted camper. The friend had flown home, but Paul was still there, about to start work in a cannery.

The *Fearless* left Skagway with Paul on board, fuel tanks topped off, and quarters stocked. It was a bright, even joyous, brimming July day as they maneuvered past Sullivan Island. While his boat made the run down Lynn Canal, Bob tuned the radar and depth sounder, and because the sun was out on a fair afternoon, and the green water lay sleek and glassy, and because his new deckhand seemed stalwart and reliable, he felt—for the first time since May, really—good about things. In this state of mind, he went outside, made his way forward, and peered up toward the pilothouse window, where Paul—he would not forget this—stood tall at the wheel. Paul nodded at him gravely, as if he'd been piloting the *Fearless* for years, then fixed his gaze once again to the southeast and the promise of the Chatham Strait fishing grounds.

There was a net closure, and for a few days they trolled for silvers. They worked the rip at Point Gardner for a dozen modest fish; they dragged twenty-two fathoms off Admiralty Island for two dozen more. Paul learned to gaff fish behind the gills to avoid damaging the meat. Bob showed him how to work the gurdies and how to unsnap the leaders as they came up with their spoons and how to coil them neatly in the stern. Then came a twenty-four-hour gillnet opening. They fished a tight corner with the Port Protection fleet, the tide running hard, the boats close to one another, the evening westerly tossing spray across the pilothouses. In the dark, Paul picked his first net clean—sixty-five chums in a stiff night wind beneath the season's first northern lights. The moon went down, and they fished the beach with the radar, running in tight and dropping the net light, then plowing out again and dropping net off the drum. They drifted through a kelp bed, with Paul tossing fish in the hold and kelp over the gunnels. He was definitely paying off—a good deckhand.

Paul, Bob said, spoke sometimes about high-school football and wrestling. He claimed he could play the guitar, but regretted his lack of seriousness about it. He wasn't sure about college. He thought he might do something else—he didn't know what. He confessed to confusion about his future and said that, so far, the worst thing about fishing was no women. He'd really liked women, Bob said.

In August, Paul confronted evil weather. They set the net in a heavy rain, a big wind driving seawater across both decks. A gale came up, the tide ebbed hard, and Bob decided to reel up and slip into a bight in the shoreline. But the high speed in the reel drive quit against the tide with the net still two-thirds in the water. In the storm, with the wind blowing the tops off of waves and the offshore rips boiling over in overfalls and combers, the *Fearless* towed her net beyond Cape Lynch, where the tide swept her out to open water. The clutch quit working inside of fifteen minutes, and Paul and Bob pulled net by hand. They took turns. They worked in their rain gear, with the sea coming from all directions. Darkness fell, and the sea steepened; the *Fearless* cupped deeply into westerly swells, and Bob had to get behind the wheel. Paul pulled net on his own for four hours. Afterward, when Bob complimented him for sticking it out solo, Paul answered that sticking it out was something his father had trained into him.

Weather prevented them from making the run south, and for three days they waited it out at Twin Coves, holed up and reading novels. Bob brought out his bag of marijuana. Paul recollected, aloud, high-school girls. He explained how he'd stolen, on a regular basis, cases of beer from delivery trucks. He said that after graduating from high school he'd gone into the mountains for two weeks with a guy from football. This was the guy he'd driven to Alaska with—now in California, pouring asphalt.

Paul said he was rethinking everything. Football, for example, and wrestling—he'd never liked either one. Why had he done those things? What was the point? And what would he do now? Where would he live? He wanted to go far away, he said. He wanted to go to South America. He wanted to learn to lay tile, too. He wanted to build a post-and-beam barn. He thought he might ride a bicycle across the country. He showed Bob some genuinely mystifying card tricks. He had an idea for a movie, he said, that would include optical illusions and levitation, and he believed it was possible to make Mars habitable. He was eager to learn how to scuba-dive.

"Now comes the hard part," Bob said.

They lay at anchor at Twin Coves in sixty-knot winds and twelve-foot seas; the wipers froze solid, and ice formed in the rigging. In a lull, they made the run to Point Horton, but the radar locked up when they were less than midway, and they had to jog for twelve hours through a snowstorm. Finally, though, they made Ketchikan, where they paired up with the *Wayfarer*—another gillnetter—for the run across Dixon Entrance. The two boats lit south, running for home, but more ill weather blew down from the north, and they had to lay anchor in Customhouse Cove with snow freezing against the pilothouse windows. Once again, the rigging iced up; the radio reported steepening seas and a fifty-five-knot gale. Then, on the third day, the forecast called for clearing, and the skippers agreed to run for it at first light.

At three in the morning, Bob flicked on the radar and stared for a long time at the empty scope while Paul slept in the fo'c'sle. A rough squall passed through Customhouse Cove, and, in his rain gear, reluctantly, Bob went out to let slip more anchor chain. At dawn, they pushed off for Foggy Bay with the *Wayfarer* to port and in radio contact; they cleared Mary Island and plowed into the vast just as the Coast Guard broadcast a gale warning for the length of the northern coast. Bob radioed the *Wayfarer,* but since the seas in front of them were apparently calm, she radioed back to say she would run for Foggy Bay at least. There was time, her skipper said, before the wind came up.

The *Fearless* followed, quartering to stern, but the wind, a northerly, came in at seven-thirty. The water darkened. The tops of the swells blew off all around, so that shreds of foam flew past. The seas grew tall, and the two boats jogged in tandem to put their trolling poles down. The last of the flood came at eight-fifteen, and as the tide turned back against the wind, the sea rolled even higher. It rolled over both decks of the *Fearless* so deeply that Bob had to send Paul down to clear the bilges while he, at the wheel, negotiated swells, first from the west and then from the south, with the southwest chop and the tide pushing on top. The waves pressed so hard against the windows the glass sagged with their weight. Water poured in over the stern, filled the cockpit, and drained as the boat throttled uphill. Once, to port, Bob caught a glimpse of the *Wayfarer,* a third of her keel visible as she rode the waves. When he turned to look starboard, Paul stood beside him with a strand of vomit hanging from his mouth. "Taking a quick break," he explained.

Bob had passed storms at the bilges himself, clearing the strainers of wet cardboard and caked oil, wedged in tight alongside the engine, listening to its scream, and breathing the putrid odor of diesel fumes, old salmon, and musty wood. It was not long before a person might have to vomit in that unlit and windowless hellhole. A storm would shake the entire length of the boat, and as you lay on your belly, her hull shuddered under you; you prayed with your face to the ribbing that she wouldn't go under while you were down there alone beside that slamming engine.

"You better get back down," Bob said. "I need you pumping bilge."

Paul went. Darkness came. The seas steepened. Water buried the bow to the cabin; they lost radio contact with the *Wayfarer,* but Bob could see her running lights as she mounted into a nearby wave. He kept the *Fearless* diving deep into troughs and throttled hard up the steepest hills of white water, listening to the engine change pitch. Then, in the dark, the mast and the radio antenna toppled. There was a crash and a shudder, and the *Fearless* listed to starboard, her mast hanging on by its rigging.

Paul came topside; anyone would have done that. Bob didn't blame him for abandoning his post. But as soon as Paul slid the pilothouse door open, Bob waved him off and said, "Get back out there! Cut the damn thing loose! Cut that mast loose now!"

Paul went out with a flashlight and a hatchet. It was the last time Bob saw him, alive or dead. He wore his rain gear. He went without a question. There was vomit hanging from his lip.

They were swamped by three big ones in succession. They rode low, and the engine died. The *Fearless* turned broadside and, helpless now, did a half-roll into the ocean. It seemed to Bob both sudden and inevitable; he had just enough time to drag back the pilothouse door and make a grab before the water hit him.

He stayed with the boat, clinging to a gunnel, and screamed Paul's name repeatedly. He called for a minute, and then he stopped. He adjusted his grip and hung on, silent. The lights of the *Wayfarer* cut through the sleet. She came near, her skipper made some minor adjustments—tricky and deft, given the boiling of the waves—and then her deckhand tossed out a life ring. He missed for six or seven tries before the *Wayfarer* quartered in closer. Bob hung on; he was getting numb, though. His hands no longer felt anything. The life ring came his way again. After ten or twelve more tries, he grabbed it. He let go of the gunnel and held on to the life ring. Then he was under. He came up again. The deckhand pulled him to within ten feet of the pilothouse before a wave pitched Bob onto the *Wayfarer*'s afterdeck, where he broke his nose against the net winch.

After Bob left the house that night, Hutchinson's daughter wept uncontrollably, and Hutchinson's wife consoled her. They sat together in a paralyzed embrace beside the dining-room table. Hutchinson sat with a hand on his head. They stayed like that for at least five minutes with the cold food still on the table. Then his wife and daughter rose and, limbs tangled, left the dining room together.

Hutchinson wondered if he should leave the house now. The flashlight, the hatchet, the rain gear, the vomit—he knew it was better not to imagine that. It was too real to be imagined.

He was about to leave—he'd just stood up—when Laura came in with a photo album and showed him a portrait he'd taken of Paul, seven years ago, holding a duck by its neck. Then she removed it from its plastic sleeve and passed it into his keeping. "That's yours," she said. "You take it."

"It's ours," replied Hutchinson.

He left, taking the photograph with him. A friend of his who was a trucking consolidator had an in-law apartment over his garage, and that was where Hutchinson was staying right now, but he didn't go there yet. He drove, instead, to a parking lot at a mall, found a lonely spot there, pushed his seat back, shut his eyes, and leaned his head against the window. Twelve, he thought—Paul had been twelve. He opened his eyes and looked at the photograph. Paul had on not only his checked coat but, under it, two wool sweaters.

He knew the spot where this photograph was taken. You drove under power lines beside a little feeder stream that sometimes had mallards in it. When he went there with Paul, everything was frozen over. They'd had to break ice in order to set out the decoys.

He remembered what happened. It was snowing that day. They were back in the reeds. Snow landed on the shoulders of their coats and settled on their caps and on the decoys. The wind blew it, stinging, into their faces. Flights of ducks would suddenly appear in it, the whistling of their wings and their cries long preceding them. It was fast shooting, and Paul missed his shots. Then a single greenhead came low across a point of sedge, and Paul fired straight on, then going-over, and then a long going-away that caused the duck to arc steeply to the ice, where it flopped for a while before settling.

The dog picked it up. Enough was enough. It was late in the day; it was starting to get dark. They walked back to the truck, where Hutchinson got his camera. Paul held the duck by the neck for this picture. "Smile," Hutchinson had said, from behind the viewfinder. He remembered that Paul had tried to smile—his face contorting, searching for the right shape. "Come on," urged Hutchinson, "smile a little." But it hadn't happened—it was not a real smile—and Hutchinson had been forced to snap the picture with his son's face arranged in this false way.

Hush

"Lou Calhoun?" she said into her phone.

"Who wants to know?"

"Eastside Pet Care."

"Joker," the guy answered.

"I walk dogs. Your friend gave me your number."

"You walk dogs."

"Professionally."

"My friend? Which friend?"

"Jim and Joan Jarvis. They said you wanted me to call."

"I'm being worked here."

"No, you're not."

"You have a business license?"

"No."

"Who are you?"

"Vivian Lee."

"What's the accent?"

Vivian said, "Mississippi. Long time ago."

There was a pause. "Ma-sippi," said Lou Calhoun. "A Mississippi dog walker. Mississippi dog walker—never heard of that before."

"Shit happens," answered Vivian. Because it had.

There was a laugh at the other end that turned into a cough. "Three references," said Lou Calhoun. "I'll call back, depending. Got my pencil ready, so shoot."

He called two days later. He said, "Sounds good, except you charge a lot."

"No."

"I called around," said Lou. "You charge a lot."

"Okay."

"You got any questions?"

"What kind of dog?"

"I got a Rottweiler, old. Walks like a champ, though."

His house was hard to find. A cemetery interfered with the continuity of addresses. She had to snake around the back of it, contending with speed bumps, on streets cracked and buckled by hoary roots and littered with dropped catkins. Lou's house turned out to be conspicuously new, given the mossy neighborhood. He had a no-maintenance yard, all gravel and beauty bark, and some bonsai trees in pots that either needed water or were dead already. She went up the walk, but before she could ring the doorbell, Lou's voice came out of an intercom. "I know you're there," it said.

She waited. The Rottweiler started barking at her from inside the door. It sounded incorrigible. Then, from the intercom, "I'm buzzing you in now." The latch hummed next, but instead of going in, Vivian pushed the intercom's speaker button and yelled, "I'm not walking in on that dog."

"His name's Bill. Bill's all talk. Walk in and say hi to him."

"No."

After a while, Lou's garage door rose. Then she heard him, again, on the intercom. "On-tray," he said. "You're safe."

There was a station wagon in Lou's garage, which otherwise looked like the site of a junk sale—tables of clothing, dishware, knickknacks, paperback books, a corner full of lamps, a lot of videocassettes, a collection of old phones and answering machines in a nest of snarled cord and wire. A door opened, and there was Lou, leaning on an aluminum walker. He looked like Kirk Douglas—the liver spots, the sunburn, the helmet of gray hair, the long earlobes, the puffy eyelids, the hole in his chin. "Holy moly," he said.

Vivian didn't answer.

"I didn't know they were going to send a looker. Bill's harmless," he added.

"Right," said Vivian, who was forty-three.

"There's a leash over there," said Lou. "Will you get it?"

She got the leash. Bill was still barking, somewhere in the house. "I locked him up," said Lou. "Come in for just a minute. I got a muzzle he has to wear in public. My hip," he added, and began a deliberate rotation, slow to the point of painful to watch, on the points of his walker. "You go ahead of me," he ordered.

Vivian did. Lou made struggling noises. "Turn right," he gasped. "Bill! Pipe down!"

They made it to the living room. Lou had a large television. His floor made a din under his walker that mingled with the din from Bill. "Tell me your name again," Lou said.

"Vivian Lee."

"How'd you end up walking dogs?"

"I'm a country song."

"Which?"

"All of them."

"Drunk, broke, driftin', divorced, half dead, just outa jail, hungover, beat up, cheated on, and—a cheater yourself."

"Fifty percent of that. Approximately." She meant, though, broke at the moment and cheated on repeatedly.

"Which fifty?"

"Doin' menial for folks."

"Ha," said Lou. "You can't get no respect." He shrugged and wiped his sweaty forehead with his wrist. "All right," he said. "So what's our agreement?"

"I walk your dog."

"I'm not going to sit," Lou said. "Up and down's too much. What's our agreement?"

"Monday, Wednesday, Friday."

"The rate?"

She told him.

"Pipe down!" Lou yelled again. "Hey, Bill! Shut up!"

Bill stopped. He made a whine that sounded like the air going out of him. This was followed by low, menacing noises—attenuated growls, chippy barks, clawing at a door. "Muzzle," said Lou. "Let me get it."

"Muzzle?" she answered. "Do I really want to walk your dog?"

"At your rate, absolutely. Like I said, he's a cream puff." Lou made an effort to sweep-groom his hair, but what he

really needed was two hands on his walker. "Muzzle," he said.
"I gotta find his muzzle." Again he made a tedious rotation.
"Where is it?" asked Vivian. "I'll get it."

They made a foray toward the kitchen. "Slim possibility,"
Lou said. "Things collect there." She went ahead of him down
a hall, and he called, "Just a minute, hold up, hold on, slow
down, wait," and, when they arrived—referring to empty
containers—"I have to do Meals on Wheels right now, that's
their stuff." From the sink windowsill, a tiny radio emitted
talk; the subject was government spending; someone was calling in. There was an issue of *Forbes* and a squeezable honey
bear on the table, but no muzzle.

"Maybe you can walk him without it," said Lou. "He
doesn't always need it. Just, if you see another dog, cross the
street. Muzzle isn't necessary."

"Forbes," Vivian said.

"You keep up with finance?"

"Not really," said Vivian. "Despite my exorbitant dog-
walking rates."

Lou grinned. "Put your money in CDs," he said. "FDIC-
insured. You know FDIC rules?" With his chin, he indicated
his chattering radio. There were plastic flowers beside it in a
vase. "Listen to these jerks," he said. "Yay-hoos."

"Meals on Wheels?" asked Vivian.

"Scuzz," Lou said. "You get gouged so they can kill you
with salt and cholesterol. But it's not Meals on Wheels, it's
something else."

"Someone does the cooking."

"The chef who does rubber chicken for luncheons." Lou

raised his walker and banged it on the floor. "Do I look like I need a bib?" he wondered. "Fuck it," he added. "Bill."

"Bill," said Vivian. "Muzzle or no muzzle?"

"We'll get him suited up," answered Lou.

They wound through the house. There was a mudroom in back, and Bill was sequestered there, still making neurotic and murderous noises. Lou blocked him with the walker and said, "Up, you jerk, get up here, Bill," and the dog immediately put its paws on the walker so that Lou could attach the leash to its collar. Vivian saw immediately that Bill wore a choke collar—chain links and a ring—and also a studded ID collar. He was a huge salivator with big green eyes. "Look," said Lou. "It's staring us in the face." He meant the muzzle, in front of him, on a hook. "That's where I keep it," he said. "Can you grab it?"

Vivian did, which provoked a growl from Bill. "Hey, shut up," Lou hissed.

He got the muzzle on. Then he gave Vivian the leash. "Go out this door," he said. "You know the neighborhood?"

"No."

"Go left—I go left. Bill likes to do his duty in the cemetery. You know the cemetery?"

With the wire cage over his snout, Bill seemed subdued. He sat there panting. Lou touched his head. "Piece a shit," he said. "Get out of here."

Wednesday came. Same drill—intercom, garage door, a half-hour of fussing, going in circles. Vivian walked Bill again. Outfitted in his preventative gear, he was a cinch, meek. He heeled perfectly, and performed discreetly in the cemetery. On

Friday, Lou had an article for Vivian, cut from a magazine and folded sharply in half. "Getting Started in Small Business." In the upper right corner he'd scrawled the magazine's name, as well as the article's date of publication. Lou's handwriting was shaky and archaic. "You need this," he said. "It's the basics."

"I'll take a look."

Lou gestured magnanimously. "Don't look," he said. "Read it."

Vivian read it over the weekend. "You were right," she told Lou on Monday. "To start, I'm getting licensed, bonded, and insured."

"I told you," Lou said.

"After that," said Vivian, "my rates go up. They'll have to—I'm adding costs."

"Joker," answered Lou.

Each week, Lou had new troubles. His eyeballs looked yellow—in fact, one eyeball now looked bigger than the other. Something in his gut was infected, and whatever it was, it made him slower. His feet swelled. He told Vivian he had a ringing in his ears. His teeth looked darker, except they weren't his teeth, they were a bridge, she could see, supported by gold crowns. Lou's doctor told him not to eat anything fatty, not to have a drink, and not to do anything stupid. Meanwhile, he had pills in a dispenser with space for a thirty-day run— plus, he had to take a cab to the pharmacy, because his hip couldn't handle it when he got behind the wheel. Groceries? Impossible. How would you get down the aisle with a cart? What were you supposed to do with your bags when it was time to carry them out to the cab? On the other hand, Meals on Wheels for breakfast, lunch, and dinner? Insane bills. A minor freebie: he had a friend who lent him videos, so he was watching a lot of flicks he'd missed. Over the last weekend, he'd run through *The Hunt for Red October, The Godfather Part III, Pretty Woman,* and *Dances with Wolves.*

"Dinner on Wheels and a movie," said Vivian. "The good life."

"Pathetic."

"What about other needs?"

"Now you're talking," said Lou.

"I mean toilet paper," said Vivian. "Going to the post office."

"Yes, I wipe my ass," said Lou. "I got housecleaning service for the bathrooms, the rugs. I—"

"Say you need dog food," Vivian countered. "Who goes for dog food?"

"I'm fine."

Lou had Crohn's disease. He had to have a colostomy. For a while he banished his dog to a holding pen. But then Bill needed walking again. Lou told Vivian it might be time to find Bill another home, because the jerk spent all his time barking and growling. Something was wrong with his fur—there were holes in it. "Bare patches," said Lou. "He needs a vet. Maybe I'll have to put a gun to his head. Fucking Bill," said Lou. "You little bastard."

It was Vivian who finally took Bill to a vet. Bill had the mange. He had other problems, too—a heart murmur, wheezy lungs. Vivian had to call Lou to okay Bill's pills. "What are my options?" Lou asked her.

"You could have him put down."

"Have him put down or spend money on the son of a bitch," said Lou. "All right, go ahead, blow money on dog pills. I like to throw good money after bad."

Lou had kids from two marriages—two boys—and a granddaughter. "I got a problem with Boy Two," he told Vivian. "He's an alkie, and I don't approve of his lifestyle. Boy One's a frigging straight arrow, but he's pissed off at me or something. My granddaughter, it's different, whatever she does is good. I mean whatever she does—it doesn't matter—but she's in Guam. She actually lives in Guam. It's like Mars. And it presents me with these out-a-sight logistical problems. Why couldn't she be like other people's grandkids and live in California? I know what I sound like," Lou said. "You got kids?"

"Boy. Twenty. Living with his dad and doing nothing right now that I can see."

"Ought to go to college," said Lou. "You ever fly to Guam?"

"No."

"I'll impress this on you. It's moon travel."

"Thanks."

"How she stands it, I don't know," said Lou. "I'm starting to think she might be a lesbian. You know how I can tell?"

"No."

"I can't. She doesn't make it obvious. But it's between the lines for me. There's omissions."

Another thing: finances were starting to drive Lou crazy. He had mutual funds, but he would read so much about them—prospectuses, reports—that he lost faith. He had annuities, but they irritated him, he said, "because they're behind the ball." The statements Lou got from banks and insurance companies, from Charles Schwab and the IRS—all of it had to be organized and entered into Quicken, but his screen gave Lou headaches. "Look at my eyes," he told Vivian. "Look close. They're bloodshot. I got these bags now, double bags, I gotta take my brows between my fingers and lift them up because they're hanging in my eyes. And my so-called computer. It does its own thing. I had a guy here three months ago to clean up the so-called hard drive, but as far as I can tell, I'm back where I started. Call Hewlett-Packard sometime. You call Hewlett-Packard, you're on the phone till Christmas. They don't want to help you; it costs them too much. What I'm saying is obvious. I don't have to say it. The idea is to bog you down till you surrender. These people are excellent. They evaporate. Poof."

Bill slowed down. He was phlegmy, and he hacked. Lou became philosophical about him. "Congestive heart failure," he told Vivian. "He's all backed up. His lungs are drowning. Poor fuck," he said, "he's shitting on the floor now. I've had it up to here with him. Bill's become a pill. It's probably time for him to go kaput. What do you think? What's your opinion?"

"Maybe," said Vivian.

She heard more complaining. Doctors were a source of anguish. "Just because they went to medical school, they now have the right to treat you like shit? Doctor comes in, I make him slow down. I chew his ear off. Come on, let's *talk* a little. My theory is, you see sick people every day, pretty soon it's a living, even if you're an idealist, even if you think you want to save the world. You see *Soylent Green*?"

"No."

"You were like six when *Soylent Green* came out. This movie, they invent a 'Soylent Green.' It's what people eat. And it's made from geriatrics. You get old, they turn you into— what do they call it—food staples."

"Something to look forward to."

"Shit," said Lou.

Bill died in the mudroom. Vivian wrapped him in an army blanket Lou had in his garage and dropped him at the vet. When she came back, Lou was drinking Crown Royal. "What else?" she asked. "Are you good?"

"I don't get sentimental about canines," Lou growled. "I've had seven now, all gone to doggie heaven. I'm drinking in front of you. You want a drink? In there's the liquor cabinet. You know where it is. I don't claim to have clean glasses around here. Help yourself, take what you want. To Bill," he added. "That fucker."

"To Bill."

"It doesn't count if you don't have a drink."

"Fine," said Vivian. "I'll have one."

Lou had decent gin. She poured some over ice. They sat in the living room, facing the picture window, with its view of bark and gravel and of the house across the street. "This is nice of you," said Lou. "I'll pay you extra."

"Do you get weeds in your beauty bark?"

"Do I get weeds in my beauty bark."

"Growing up, I never saw beauty bark," said Vivian.

"They started having it, I don't know, a while ago, I guess. So what did the vet say?"

"I didn't see the vet."

"What's the scenario?"

"They just took him. I don't know."

"If I wasn't such an invalid, I'd have buried his royal ass. Save a few dollars, turn him into dirt."

"My guess is, they cremate."

"With horses," explained Lou, "they turn them into dog food. So maybe they'll turn fucking Bill into horse food. I spent time in China, and that's all a myth. No one eats dogs there. It's not on the menu. You want to know something? The Germans were eating dogs—I was there. People were eating shoe leather. Whores were a nickel. And people like to say it was the so-called good war. We did Japan about a year before my wife went—a year and three months. We checked out Hiroshima—you want to get depressed? And that was a drop in the bucket by comparison. In my opinion, the dooms-day clock is running. But that's someone else's problem—I'm checking out. Hey," said Lou. "Don't forget." He raised his glass. "Here's to Fuckface."

"I have to say, he looked great in that muzzle."

"Bill was stand-up," Lou insisted. "I loved his attitude. I admired his bullshit. He'd tear the door down. He'd kill you for looking at him. He had this thing he did with his face." Lou snarled, curling his upper lip. " 'I'm Bill, don't cross me, I'll tear your throat out. I'll rip your head off.' Fucking king of the jungle. Actually, Bill was a junkyard dog—did I tell you this? I got him from the pound. He was beat down, a slinker. My wife used to give him raw hamburger, with salt."

"To Bill," said Vivian. They drank.

For a moment, neither of them knew what to say. "You don't have to stay here," Lou said. "It's not like I'm in mourning."

"Right."

"Fucking dog," said Lou.

"Maybe you can get another."

"What for?" said Lou. "You angling for work?"

"Just carrying a conversation. 'You can always get another dog.' That's my line, I have to say it."

"True."

"But the next dog should be smaller."

"You sound like my wife. Harangue, harangue. Needle, needle, needle. Take out the garbage. Get another dog. And make sure it's a smaller dog—a smaller dog, Louis!" Lou again brought his glass to his lips. "Nostalgia," he said. "At least I still remember shit. You heard of transient global amnesia?"

"No."

"I got it," said Lou. "One out of approximately thirty-five thousand people gets it, and I got it. You're just sitting there. It could happen right now—you're sitting there, nothing special, no warning, bang, you don't know where you are or how you got there. This is one of those things," said Lou. "On top of everything else. I know I'm me, knock on wood, I'm me, but the room? The site? The venue? The place? I could literally be anywhere. I'm lost—I'm clueless. I was told this can happen from blowing your nose. Something as stupid as blowing your nose. The type where you pinch your nostrils closed? They say you can get it from diving into cold water. From sex, I mean, Jesus. Hey, what about that? From vigorous sex, you don't know where you are? I told them I was willing to do that experiment, free of charge, for the good of science."

"Hmmm."

"Old guy babbling bullshit," said Lou. "Let me pay you now, so you can go."

Vivian said, "On angling for work. For other clients, I do errands and odd jobs. Whatever they need. So, if you decide you want some help with something." Vivian shrugged. "I'm available."

"Nah," said Lou. "I don't need any help."

He called a day later. "I thought of something," he said. "You charge the same rates if it's not dog walking?"

"What is it?"

"Let's confirm the rate first."

"Yes—the same."

"Okay," said Lou. "I need someone to drive over to UPS and pick up a package they're holding."

"What?"

"Just a package."

"I'm not getting involved in anything illegal."

"Come on," said Lou. "I'm geriatric here. The most illegal thing I get into is cutting tags off of mattresses. With dull scissors."

She did the errand. He gave her a solid tip. In the package was a new lightweight walker, which she assembled. "Fuck," said Lou, trying it out. "This is bullshit."

"Don't give up."

"Who are you—Winston Churchill? I thought you were Ma-sippi. Hey," he said. "There's one more thing. Come in here for a minute. In the kitchen."

She unstuck the ice maker by putting a screwdriver up a slot and pushing something. "Another thing," said Lou. She cleaned the lint trap in his dryer. "One more," said Lou. "It'll only take a second." She started the station wagon's engine so its battery wouldn't die. "I'd do it myself," said Lou, "but you gotta pump that pedal. I ought to sell the thing—it's like owning a bus. My wife used it. I used to take the seats out and cram it full of crap. You want to buy a station wagon?"

"No."

"I'll give you a deal."

"Do you need help selling your car?" asked Vivian. "I can put an ad in the paper, show it, you sign the title, it's gone."

"Maybe," answered Lou. "Let me think about that."

He sent her to the library. He wanted her to look up Blue Book on the station wagon and make a copy of the page. She was supposed to look for three books he wanted, two on investing and one called *Fly Cheap!* "I need to drag my ass to Guam," he said. "One of these days. Guess what? My granddaughter's pregnant."

"I thought she was a lesbian."

"I think it's artificial insemination."

"She doesn't say?"

"She won't say."

"That's great," said Vivian. "Congratulations. That's wonderful."

"I don't know if it's so wonderful," said Lou. "Who the hell knows who the father is?"

Vivian didn't answer.

Lou was hospitalized that week: gut complications. But he got out again the next month. He called and said, "Vivian, it's me, Lou. Back from the dead. Remember me, Lou? With the Rottweiler?"

"Hi."

"I'm still alive. Missing a few parts, but alive—alive and kicking."

"Way to go, Lou. That's good. I'm happy."

"Got a query for you. You do medical? Like a nurse—medical stuff?"

"No," said Vivian. "I don't do medical."

"Because for medical your rates would be good," observed Lou. "For home care. This and that. Medical stuff. I've got problems and limitations. I gotta have help. As humiliating as it is, it's gotta happen."

"I'm sorry."

"Is that a dismissal?"

"I just don't do medical."

"Some of my stuff's easy. Errands. Like before."

"Call me for those things."

"I am calling," said Lou. "Where do I start? I got a list made up. You want me to read it to you? I'll read it to you."

"Read."

"I don't have it next to me. I'll have to get up."

"Forget it," said Vivian. "Don't get up."

It turned out Lou had colon cancer, tumors pressing on his colon from all directions—"a lot of them, like thirty," he said. He needed special bedsheets, special bed pads, an ozone machine, and a visorlike reading magnifier, which, together, took Vivian half a day to locate. He wanted a certain shampoo and certain razors. For his letters of complaint to doctors and insurers he wanted heavy bond paper, with a letterhead of his design in an intimidating font, from Copy Mart. He wanted certain stamps, the ones with flags, and business envelopes, the ones you couldn't see through. There was a wasp nest under an eave which she could bat down early in the morning, if she was willing to risk it, before the wasps got surly. Vivian hit it with a broom. She sold the station wagon for Lou—all he had to do was sign the paperwork. He broke his glasses—she got him new ones. She shopped his quirky lists—pepperoni sticks, Häagen-Dazs, mouse poison, talcum powder. She got familiar with the rotating home-care nurses, Jean, Toni, and Barb, and the housecleaner, Esmerelda. Jean had a wandering left eye and, because of extra weight, often sounded out of breath. Nothing fazed her, not even Lou's colostomy bag. When Vivian asked about it, Jean said, "I don't know. It's just not gross."

"That's all?"

"Yeah."

"A colostomy bag?"

"I guess."

"It doesn't gross you out?"

"No," said Jean.

"That I don't get," said Vivian.

Lou went into a hospice. There was no more to do. The granddaughter from Guam came in and took over. Vivian met her with an invoice in hand, because the granddaughter had power of attorney. She wasn't pregnant, but Vivian didn't ask about that. Vivian thought the granddaughter might be partly Samoan. She looked like a boxer but dressed like a barfly. "I hope Lou didn't come on to you," she told Vivian. "He's a dirty old man. It's embarrassing."

"No."

A week passed, and then Vivian did something out of character. On a whim, not intending to, she went to see Lou at his hospice. He was almost dead. He was on his side, with his face turned toward the wall. In fact, his face was touching the wall, which didn't seem right to her. "Why aren't they taking better care of him?" she thought. She tried moving his head for him by pulling on his pillow. It stirred Lou a little—small bubbles formed at his lips, and then his tongue slid out of his mouth like a dead fish. Lou said, "Uuhhhhh," followed by sleepy gurgling. They'd taken his bridge out, but he still looked like Kirk Douglas. Vivian sat in a chair pulled close to Lou's bed. There was nothing to do. There was no reason to be here. What could you say to someone who was dying: Don't worry? Relax? It's all good? No problem? She remembered Kirk Douglas in a movie called *The Vikings*. She must have been ten or so, at the theater in Leland—the Rex, she remembered, sixty-five cents. They put him on a ship and shot it full of flaming arrows. Going out like a Viking. This hospice wasn't that. In fact, what was happening to Lou seemed terribly ignominious. He didn't even have a window, she noticed. He was dying to the tune of his own smell here. And he was dying alone. Where was that granddaughter? Where were the straight-arrow and the alkie sons? Vivian said, "Hey, Lou, are you there, can you hear me?" She shook him next, but touched his covers, not him. "Lou!" she said, and he gurgled again. What did it mean, this gurgling he was doing? Was he trying to communicate from a hundred leagues under? If so, it must be something important. "Lou!" she said again. "It's me, Vivian Lee. If you've got something to say, you should go ahead and say it." And, holding her nose, she put an ear to his lips. "I wuv you," whispered Lou, bridgeless, doped up.

Vivian sat back. This was something to think about,

because she didn't want to say the wrong thing in reply. Her words could be the last words he heard. Between now and the time he shut down completely, Lou was going to be thinking about them—maybe. The thoughts of a dying man— that was one of the few remaining mysteries. The moon was mapped, the Voyager probe was beyond Neptune, Robert Ballard had visited the *Titanic*—but what was Lou thinking right now, while he died? One thing for sure, he was down to just thoughts, there was nothing else, so her answer could be important. Erring on the side of caution, then, Vivian said, "Hush." By which she meant what? She didn't know, actually. "Hush," she said again, but it wasn't enough. She needed to say more, she needed to explain it—she who walked dogs and did errands for rich people. "At least I wasn't nothing in your eyes," she said, then put a hand on Lou's wrist and squeezed it. "Hush," she said, one more time.

A NOTE ABOUT THE AUTHOR

David Guterson is the author of five novels: *Snow Falling on Cedars,* which won the PEN/Faulkner and the American Booksellers Association Book of the Year Award; *East of the Mountains; Our Lady of the Forest,* a *New York Times* Notable Book and a *Los Angeles Times* and *Seattle Post-Intelligencer* Best Book of the Year; *The Other;* and *Ed King.* He is also the author of a previous story collection, *The Country Ahead of Us, the Country Behind;* a poetry collection, *Songs for a Summons;* and two works of nonfiction, *Family Matters: Why Homeschooling Makes Sense* and *Descent: A Memoir of Madness.* A recipient of a Guggenheim Fellowship, he lives in Washington State.

A NOTE ON THE TYPE

This book was set in Granjon, a type named in compliment to Robert Granjon, a type cutter and printer active in Antwerp, Lyons, Rome, and Paris from 1523 to 1590. Granjon, the boldest and most original designer of his time, was one of the first to practice the trade of typefounder apart from that of printer.

Linotype Granjon was designed by George W. Jones, who based his drawings on a face used by Claude Garamond (ca. 1480–1561) in his beautiful French books. Granjon more closely resembles Garamond's own type than do any of the various modern faces that bear his name.

Composed by North Market Street Graphics,
Lancaster, Pennsylvania

Printed and bound by Berryville Graphics,
Berryville, Virginia

Designed by Cassandra J. Pappas